Marrying Mr. English

THE ENGLISH BROTHERS, BOOK #7
THE BLUEBERRY LANE SERIES

KATY REGNERY

Marrying Mr. English
Copyright © 2015 by Katharine Gilliam Regnery

Excerpt from the letter of Robert Browning to Elizabeth Barrett Browning in *The Letters of Robert Browning and Elizabeth Barrett Browning: 1845–1846* by Robert Browning and Elizabeth Barrett Browning.

Excerpt from the poem "Spring Carol" in *New Poems and Variant Readings* (1918) by Robert Louis Stevenson.

Excerpts from *Lady Chatterley's Lover* by D.H. Lawrence.

Excerpt from "Sonnet 7" in *Sonnets from the Portuguese* by Elizabeth Barrett Browning.

Please visit www.katyregnery.com

First Edition: December 2015
Katy Regnery

Marrying Mr. English: a novel / by Katy Regnery—1st ed.
ISBN: 978-1-63392-078-1

Library of Congress Cataloging-in-Publication Data available upon request

Published in the United States by Spencer Hill Press
This is a Spencer Hill Contemporary Romance, Spencer Hill
Contemporary is an imprint of Spencer Hill Press.
For more information on our titles visit www.spencerhillpress.com

Distributed by Midpoint Trade Books
www.midpointtrade.com

Cover design by: Marianne Nowicki
Interior layout by: Scribe Inc.
The World of Blueberry Lane Map designed by: Paul Siegel

Printed in the United States of America

The Blueberry Lane Series

THE ENGLISH BROTHERS

Breaking Up with Barrett
Falling for Fitz
Anyone but Alex
Seduced by Stratton
Wild about Weston
Kiss Me Kate
Marrying Mr. English

THE WINSLOW BROTHERS

Bidding on Brooks
Proposing to Preston
Crazy about Cameron
Campaigning for Christopher

THE ROUSSEAUS

Jonquils for Jax
Coming August 2016

Marry Me Mad
Coming September 2016

J.C. and the Bijoux Jolis
Coming October 2016

THE STORY SISTERS

Four novels
Coming 2017

THE AMBLERS

Three novels
Coming 2018

Based on the best-selling series by Katy Regnery,

The World of...

Blueberry Lane

The Rousseaus of Chateau Nouvelle
Jax, Mad, J.C.
Jonquils for Jax • Marry Me Mad
J.C and the Bijoux Jolis

The Story Sisters of Forrester
Priscilla, Alice, Elizabeth, Jane
Coming Summer 2017

The Winslow Brothers of Westerly
Brooks, Preston, Cameron, Christopher
Bidding on Brooks • Proposing to Preston
Crazy About Cameron • Campaigning for Christopher

The Amblers of Greens Farms
Bree, Dash, Sloane
Coming Summer 2018

The English Brothers of Haverford Park
Barrett, Fitz, Alex, Stratton, Weston, Kate
Breaking up with Barrett • Falling for Fitz
Anyone but Alex • Seduced by Stratton
Wild about Weston • Kiss Me Kate
Marrying Mr. English

For my own mother and father, who have a
breathtaking love story of their own.
I love you.

And for Henry.
Because he asked.
And because I love him tons.

CONTENTS

Prologue

"Once upon a time . . ."

Chapter 1

Vail, Colorado
December 1981

"C'mon, Ellie," pleaded Eve Marie. "They're, like, rich."

"They're *all* rich," said Eleanora Watters, hustling into the kitchen of Auntie Rose's Breakfast-All-Day Chalet with an armload of dirty plates.

Eve Marie followed her through the swinging door.

"But they seem *ni-i-i-ice*," she whined.

"They *all* seem nice," said Eleanora over her shoulder, nodding at Manny as he took the dirty dishes and winked at her.

"But these two really *are*."

Eleanora turned to face her younger cousin, pushing a stray lock of blonde hair behind her ear and planting her fists on her hips. "Like the last ones? And the ones before them?"

Eve Marie had the decency to look embarrassed.

"When are you going to learn, Evie? They're all rats. Rich, old, entitled, grabby rats. They come to Vail looking for a young waitress or hotel maid to warm up their bed for a week, and once they've had their fun, they leave. Do you know *who* they leave?"

"Us," said Eve Marie dolefully.

"Us," confirmed Eleanora. "And are we harlots to be thusly used?"

Eve Marie screwed up her face in confusion.

Eleanora rolled her eyes, rephrasing, "Are we hos, cuz?"

"No," said Eve Marie, though there wasn't much conviction in her voice.

"No, we are not," said Eleanora crisply. "We deserve better than that, Evie."

Images of home flashed through her mind at lightning speed before she could stop them: *her father's grubby double-wide, choked by a rusty chain-link fence . . . the hell-hole of a bar where her tips hadn't been worth the slow death of her dreams . . . and*—she touched Evie's cheek gently with her knuckles as a fierce burst of protectiveness flared within her—*her step-uncle's leering eyes and filthy, grabby hands.*

Eleanora dropped her hand and lifted her chin with determination. "If we keep our legs closed and our options open, we just might find it."

She turned to the warming lights and picked up two plates of pancakes and bacon for table two before bustling through the swinging door, back into Auntie Rose's main dining room. Designed to resemble a rustic ski lodge, the restaurant was a favorite of skiers and snowboarders who wanted to fill up on a hearty breakfast before hitting the slopes.

"Will you at least, like, say hello?" persisted Eve Marie at her cousin's shoulder, her voice almost drowned out by John Lennon's "(Just Like) Starting Over" blasting through the ceiling speakers.

Eleanora ignored her cousin and plastered a smile on her face as she carefully delivered the plates to the table. "Stack of hot cakes, side of oink. Bon appétit."

"Looks great," said the man on the left side of the booth, reaching for her wrist. He handled her gently but firmly, looking up into her eyes. "Now how about making it delectable by giving me your number?"

Without fighting for her imprisoned hand, Eleanora flicked her eyes over him. He was wearing a cream-colored Irish wool sweater—the type that sold in the local boutiques for hundreds of dollars—and had sunglasses in his heavily gelled hair. Vuarnet? No. Versace, she noted, glancing at the stem close to his ear. His hair was salt-and-pepper, and his eyes were lazy but hopeful as he grinned at her with what he probably believed was charm.

"My number . . . hmm." Eleanora sucked her bottom lip between her teeth, then released it with a provocative pop. "Sure. Okay."

He looked surprised but delighted, tightening his grip on her wrist to pull her closer. "Oh, yeah?"

"But which number?" said Eleanora, tapping her chin in thought. "So many to choose from . . ."

"Oh, I meant your—"

"—my age? It's twenty-two. To your what? Forty-five? Or the number of years between us? Roughly twenty-three. Or my birth date maybe? Nine, three, fifty-nine. And yours? Well, I'm guessing it ends in . . . hmm . . . *thirty-six*? How about *those* numbers? Probably not what you were looking for, though. Ooo! I know! Maybe you're one of the good ones and you've fallen madly in love with me and you want my ring size? It's a six. No. Come to think of it, you don't look like the type to buy me a ring, so how about the serial number on my father's shotgun? It's four, three, six, oh, oh, seven—"

"Forget it," said the man, his face bright red as he dropped her wrist.

"Sure thing."

"You're a bitch," he muttered, looking up at her with narrowed, angry eyes.

"Maybe. But I'm not a chump," she answered, ripping the bill from her pad and placing it on the table before turning on her white Keds and heading back toward the kitchen with Eve Marie at her heels.

Tom English watched the sassy little waitress make her way back across the bustling dining room, chuckling softly as he admired everything from the sharp way she'd taken down that dickweed to the way her tight ass swayed back and forth under the big white bow of her pink gingham dress.

"Wow!"

Pulling his eyes away from the waitress with a stab of regret, Tom looked across the table at his companion, Van, raising his eyebrows.

"Talk about sharp nails!" said Van.

Tom chuckled again, picking up his coffee cup and taking a sip of the strong brew.

Van sneered as his eyes tracked the blonde. "You couldn't pay me enough to go out with a girl like that. I don't care how hot she is. That guy had it right. Bitch on wheels!"

Tom's grin faded as he placed his mug back on the table and looked up at his friend. "I don't agree."

Van scoffed, rolling his eyes. "Are you effing kidding me?"

Tom shifted his gaze back to the kitchen, hoping for another glimpse of her. "Nope. I thought she was fairly spectacular."

"Fairly spectacular," mumbled Van, grimacing as he shook his head. "Well, you're not known for your taste in women. I hope to God she's not the friend the cute brunette was referring to."

Tom, on the other hand, desperately hoped she *was* because he had zero interest in the vacuous brunette, but that spitfire blonde? Oh, man. She was something different.

And he could sure use the distraction.

In just four days, Tom English was going to lose every cent of his fifteen-million-dollar inheritance because his fiancée, Diantha Montgomery, of the Philadelphia Montgomerys, had run off with her ski instructor, leaving Tom high and dry the night before their wedding.

It's not like he was heartbroken—he hadn't been marrying Di for love. No, theirs had been an agreement, a marriage of convenience. Tom's thirty-second birthday was in four days—on Christmas Eve—and unless he was married by the final day of his thirty-first year, his eccentric old codger of a grandfather would disown him. Tom had heard the lecture a thousand times:

A good woman makes a man honest, makes him work harder, makes him true. If you don't have a good woman in your life by age thirty-two, you don't deserve a cent and you won't get a cent. I'm not letting some devil-may-care wastrel playboy squander my millions!

Diantha, more than happy to pocket a cool million in exchange for saying "I do," had planned a lavish wedding in Vail, and they'd invited dozens of friends and family to witness the temporary nuptials. The plan was to stay married for a few months, secure Tom's inheritance, and then get a quiet divorce and go their separate ways.

But when Di didn't show up to her own rehearsal dinner last Friday, things didn't look good. A tearstained note shoved under Tom's hotel room door confirmed the rest: *Paolo and I have fallen in love and decided to elope. We're leaving for Italy tonight. I'm so sorry, T! Love, Di.*

While all the guests had returned home, Tom remained in Vail with his erstwhile best man and sometime investing partner, Edison Van Nostrand, for the week that should have been Tom's honeymoon. Time had certainly flown by with Van as their entertainment coordinator—today was Friday and Tom's birthday was Tuesday.

He shrugged and swallowed the rest of his coffee. If he was being cut off in four days, he may as well enjoy his last few days as a "devil-may-care wastrel playboy."

Van had asked their waitress—cute, airheaded brunette Eve Marie—to meet them at the bar of the Hotel Jerome tonight for some fun. The young waitress, checking out Van's brand-new Rolex, snapped her gum and offered Van a sparkling smile as she promised to "do her best" to find a friend for Tom.

Van brightened suddenly, looking over Tom's head with a lascivious grin. "Hey, angel, don't break my friend's heart and tell him *your* friend said no."

Tom shifted in his chair to find Eve Marie standing behind him, wringing her hands nervously. She blew a small bubble with her gum and sucked it back quickly, snapping it between her teeth.

"Um . . . she's not my friend; she's my cousin." She shifted her eyes from Van to Tom. "And she needs *you* to, like, answer a question first."

"Me?"

The waitress nodded at Tom, her cheeks flushing. "Yeah. She's, like, um, well . . . she needs to know your favorite book."

Without skipping a beat, Tom asked, "Fiction or nonfiction?"

This question proved a bumpy road for Eve Marie, who froze, staring blankly at Tom.

"Which one," he asked slowly, "do you think she wants to know?"

Eve Marie chewed once, then held up a single finger and hurried away. Tom watched her beeline to the feisty blonde (yes!), who was taking an order across the dining room. Tapping her cousin on the shoulder, Eve Marie cupped her hands around the blonde's ear for a moment, then leaned back expectantly. A second later, she returned to Tom.

"Fiction. Ellie said fiction."

"Now we're getting somewhere."

Tom chuckled softly, nodding at Eve Marie, who sighed happily, like she'd finally done something right.

"My favorite book of fiction. Hmm . . ."

Glancing around Eve Marie, who was twirling a long strand of teased hair around her index finger as she chewed her gum and eye-fucked Van, Tom looked across the dining room at—what had Eve Marie called her? Ellie?—Ellie, who still had her back to him, writing on her pad. Pocketing the pad, she held out her hand and collected the menus.

When she turned around, her eyes slammed into his, almost like she'd known he was staring at her all along. With the menus pressed against her chest, she stared back at him for a long moment, her posture straight, her blue eyes keen and bright. When her lips wobbled just a little, he realized she was trying not to smile, and he suddenly felt his own lips lift into a grin. But that broke the spell they were under, and she dropped his eyes quickly, heading for the kitchen and disappearing behind the swinging door without a second glance.

He didn't realize he was holding his breath until his lungs started to burn and he exhaled with a soft puff.

"Uh, Tom?" asked Van in a low voice, utterly captivated by gum-snapping, eye-fucking Eve Marie. "A book. Name a book. For the love of God, *please* name a book."

Ellie seemed brighter than average—she was quick with numbers and interested in books—but she looked young too, which meant she'd be impressionable. He considered lying. He thought about saying *A Clockwork Orange* (to seem edgy), or *The Catcher in the Rye* (to seem deep). But in the end, something about those clear, blue, unsmiling eyes made him feel ashamed of even considering deception, and he heard "*The Swiss Family Robinson*" fall from his lips instead.

Eve Marie winked at Van before looking down at Tom with glistening lips and a sexy smile. "Hmm?"

"Tell her my favorite novel is *The Swiss Family Robinson*, and ask her the name of her favorite poet."

"Uh . . . ," Eve Marie stared at him for a moment, then shrugged. "Okay. Be right back."

She sauntered away toward the kitchen, and Van adjusted his pants, grimacing. "Fuck, she's hot. How many hours is it until tonight?"

Tom looked at his watch. "About ten. But I assume you're buying her dinner first, so more like ten and a half."

"Fuck," Van muttered again. "Dinner better buy some tail."

On cue, Kenny Rogers started crooning "Lady" overhead, the lyrics *Lady, I'm your knight in shining armor and I love you* an ironic follow-up to Van's comment.

"That's real nice."

Though, judging from Eve Marie's come-hither glances, he doubted Van would have much trouble securing that tail. Him, on the other hand? He wasn't so sure. Ellie didn't look like a girl who put out as easily. Her appearance wasn't contrived to seek attention—it didn't appear that she wore makeup, and she kept her hair in a plain, tidy ponytail—and yet she was so naturally beautiful, every pair of male eyes in the room naturally gravitated toward her.

It felt like forever waiting for Eve Marie to return.

"So?" asked Tom, his anxious heart stuttering, hoping the little spitfire liked adventure fiction as much as he did.

"Elizabeth Burnett Browning," said Eve Marie.

"Barrett," he said reflexively.

"Huh?"

"Elizabeth *Barrett* Browning," said Tom.

"That's what I said."

"No, you said—"

"So, we good?" interrupted Van, leaning across the table to give Tom a look that begged him to shut the fuck up and stop arguing with the waitress he was aching to bang.

"Um, no," said Eve Marie, wrinkling her nose. "Now she needs to know your favorite *non*fiction book too."

"What the actual fuck?" exclaimed Van. "Is she a waitress or an English professor?"

Eve Marie turned away from Tom to look at Van with wide, innocent eyes. "A waitress. But she goes to college. At Colorado Mountain College over in Edwards."

"Wow," said Van sarcastically. "Colorado Mountain College! You don't say!"

"I *do* say," said Eve Marie earnestly. "She saves up her tips every month to pay for it. She's, like, supersmart."

"What does she study?" asked Tom, kicking Van under the table so he'd stop being an asshole.

"Bookkeeping," said Eve Marie. "Because math is a . . . a . . . oh, I remember! A universal language." Tom smiled at her, forcing himself not to give her a round of applause since she'd worked so hard for the answer. "But she also reads a lot of books. Ellie's, like, *always* reading books. Since as long as I've known her, and that's forever because I'm three years younger. It's, like, her favorite thing to do."

"Too bad partying isn't her favorite," said Van under his breath.

"Nope. That's *my* favorite," said Eve Marie, arching her back provocatively as she slid her gaze to Van.

Van chuckled, nodding at her with appreciation before glancing at his friend. "So, Tom, what's your all-time favorite nonfiction tome, huh?"

Tom glanced at the kitchen door, wishing Ellie would come out for a second. He'd like to look into her eyes again. He'd like to see her reaction as he answered *The Joy of Sex* or *A Moveable Feast* or . . .

He looked up at Eve Marie and grinned.

"Tell her if she wants to know my favorite nonfiction book, she has to be my date tonight."

Chapter 2

Eleanora didn't know what had prompted her to play the "What's Your Favorite Book?" game with the man at Auntie Rose's this morning, but as she and Evie walked to the Hotel Jerome at seven thirty, she had to admit that she was looking forward to this evening a lot more than the others set up by her cousin.

The Swiss Family Robinson, while not Eleanora's favorite book, was a good, honest choice, and she was curious about why he loved it. She also appreciated that he'd volleyed back, asking about her favorite poet, and she'd wondered all afternoon if he had a favorite too. Maybe tonight—instead of awkwardly sipping a club soda and leaving after an hour—she'd actually have a date worth talking to. Now wouldn't *that* be a nice turn of events?

Evie pushed through the revolving door of the hotel and walked confidently to the bar. She was familiar with all the local hotel bars, a fact that made Eleanora grimace, but she couldn't fault her cousin either. Eleanora had chosen an education as her way of bettering her life; Evie was on the fast track to love, albeit via lots and lots of quasi-anonymous sex.

"Evie," she said, placing her hand on her cousin's shoulder and making her turn around. "You don't have to sleep with him."

Evie shrugged her older cousin's hand away. "Ellie, I'm not smart like you."

Undeterred, Eleanora threaded her fingers through Evie's thick, dark hair, gently tucking a strand behind her ear. "You're sweet. And young. I worry about you."

"You're young, too," Evie said, her tone holding a reminder. Whenever Eleanora hinted about Evie's promiscuous ways, Evie countered that her cousin just didn't know how to have fun. She tilted her head to the side, grinning at Eleanora, her face bright and fearless. "Trust me. I know what I'm doing."

Then she strode into the hotel bar, leaving Eleanora to stand in the doorway on her own for a moment. The two men who'd been sitting together at Auntie Rose's several hours earlier were settled into a booth at the back, and rose as Evie approached.

The brunet, a man named Van, had already been claimed by Evie, so Eleanora looked more closely at her own date: he had a mop of sandy-blond hair and a neat mustache and wore a white button-down shirt with a tan corduroy blazer. He glanced over Evie's head and caught sight of Eleanora, a pleased smile taking over the entire real estate of his face. It was a good smile—confident and kind, interested and warm, flirtatious without being grabby. *And beautiful*, she thought, unable to look away from him as she made her way closer. *So very, very beautiful.*

"This is my cousin, Ellie," said Evie, accepting a kiss on the cheek from Van, then shimmying into the maroon leather cocktail booth beside him.

"I'm Tom," said the blond man, still holding Eleanora's eyes. "Tom English."

He didn't lean forward to kiss her, which she appreciated. It saved her the trouble of jerking back and creating an awkward moment. Instead, he held out his hand, and she saw it was wrapped in a white bandage she hadn't noticed earlier.

"You hurt yourself today, Tom," she murmured, taking his hand and pumping it very gently.

"A minor ski accident. I sprained my wrist on Devil's Dash." He chuckled with a low burr of pleasure as his fingers tightened around hers. "I'll be okay, Ellie, but thanks for worrying about me."

"Eleanora," she said. "My name isn't really Ellie—that's just what Evie calls me. My name is Eleanora Watters."

He didn't drop her hand. He didn't test out her name. He just grinned at her and nodded. "Okay."

"Ahem," said Van, and Eleanora dropped Tom's hand quickly, her face flushing as she looked down at Tom's friend. He had his arm draped around Evie's shoulders, his fingers dangling directly over her cousin's breasts, which heaved under a light pink angora sweater that covered her uniform. "Are we having drinks or what?"

Tom gestured to the booth, and Eleanora slid in next to her cousin, unwrapping her scarf and unbuttoning her coat but keeping it on. Van ordered a bottle of Asti Spumante, then leaned close to Evie and said something that made her blush and giggle. Eleanora rolled her eyes and turned to look at Tom.

"So . . ."

"So . . . ," he said, tenting his hands on the table. "Elizabeth Barrett Browning."

"Yes." Eleanora grinned at him, leaning one elbow on the table and shifting to face him. "I love her. She's so honest."

"And passionate," he added, searching her eyes thoughtfully. "Though I confess I didn't appreciate her as much as I should have when I studied her in college."

"Were you an English major?"

"I was."

"Where did you go?" she asked.

"Princeton."

Eleanora whistled low.

"You've heard of it?"

"Sure. You know Brooke Shields? From the movie *The Blue Lagoon*? She gave an interview on *The Tonight Show* and said she wants to go to Princeton someday." She swallowed, feeling a little silly, but pressing on. "So I looked it up."

"And . . . ?" he prompted, grinning at her in a way that melted any self-consciousness.

"What's not to love?"

"Your cousin said you go to college locally."

"Mm-hm." She nodded. "At Colorado Mountain College. It's hardly Princeton."

"It's still college," he said, sliding a glass of sparkling wine over to her. He held up his own glass, and Eleanora did the same. "To college. And to Elizabeth Barrett Browning."

As they sipped the sweet white wine, Eleanora felt a strange fluttering in her tummy and tried, somewhat unsuccessfully, to ignore it.

By and large, these dates were gruesome—some rich boy who wanted to get laid putting his arm around her and trying to pass off nonstop innuendo as conversation. She went for Evie's sake, in an attempt to look after her younger cousin, so that Evie didn't look all alone in the world.

But Tom English seemed different. He seemed, as Evie had indicated this morning, genuinely nice. He seemed interested in more than getting her upstairs; he was talking to her about books and college. And he was so handsome, she couldn't stop staring at him.

"What are your plans for Christmas?" she asked. "Staying here in Vail?"

"No, I'll be headed back to Philly for Christmas."

"Just here for a few days of skiing, huh?"

Her cheeks flushed hot as she heard the noise of sloppy kisses directly behind her, and she braced herself for what was coming. Any minute, her cousin would abandon her, and no matter how nice he seemed, when Tom English realized that she wouldn't be putting out like Evie, he'd make some excuse for why they should call it a night. And she'd be left to walk home alone, *again*, to her cold apartment, worried about her cousin and wishing that someone, somewhere, would see beyond the waitress uniform and want to get to know her.

"No, actually," said Tom, glancing down at his wineglass, running his index finger lazily around the rim. "I was here for . . ."

"For what?"

"To get married, actually. I got stood up."

He looked up at her then, his eyes clear and blue, unapologetic and unhurt, and that's when she felt it in her gut: she didn't care that he was older or that she was his social inferior in every possible way. She desperately hoped that right here, right now, Tom English would want to get to know her.

Tom wasn't sure what had prompted him to be so honest with her.

Maybe it was that she sat so straight, her eyes cautious, her coat still on, her blonde hair in a neat, simple ponytail, smelling faintly of maple syrup and pancakes whenever she moved her head. She was nothing like her cousin, who had one hand in Van's lap and the other raking through his scalp as they kissed noisily across the booth. Eleanora seemed like a lady—smart and pretty. No, she wasn't an East Coast debutante like Diantha or the other girls Tom had grown up with, but there was something honest and thoughtful about Eleanora Watters, and Tom hoped she wouldn't run off the moment her cousin headed upstairs with Van. He—rather desperately—hoped she'd stay and talk to him.

Van cleared his throat loudly, his voice raspy when he spoke. "I, uh, I think I left something in my room."

"I'll help you find it," said Eve Marie, jumping up to follow him.

In a flash, Van and Eve Marie were gone, leaving Tom and Eleanora with four mostly full glasses of sickeningly sweet wine and a painfully awkward silence. Would she suddenly run away without the buffer of her cousin sitting beside her? It was surprisingly and unexpectedly painful to think of losing his chance to get to know her better.

Without thinking, he reached out and grabbed her hand. "Stay and talk. That's all. Don't—don't go yet."

Her face—her very lovely face—turned to him, her pink rosebud lips tilting up in a sweet smile. She searched his face, gently pulling her hand away when she replied, "I'll stay a little longer."

It occurred to Tom that he should stop staring at her, but he couldn't. It was the first time she'd smiled at him, and his heart thundered from the way it made him feel to see her face light up. She was young and bright and ridiculously beautiful, and he'd been captivated from the first moment he'd laid eyes on her.

"*A Moveable Feast*," he said softly, memorizing the unusual blue color of her eyes, a blue somewhere between cornflower and lavender. "By Ernest Hemingway. That's my favorite nonfiction book. What's yours?"

"*How to Win Friends & Influence People*," she said. "By Dale Carnegie."

"What?" A soft laugh escaped before he could stop it. "Really?"

She nodded, grinning at him. "Uh-huh. I've read it at least six times."

"Amazing," he murmured softly. "Why?"

"Besides the fact that it's a good book?" she asked with a hint of that sass he liked so much. "Well, I hope it'll be helpful one day."

"One day when?"

"When I start my own business," she said quietly, reaching for her wineglass and taking a tiny sip.

"What kind of business?"

She shrugged. "I don't know yet. I don't—it's a long way away. Really, it's just a silly dream probably."

He searched her eyes, wondering why it wasn't more than a silly dream. She was going to college. She was obviously bright. His eyes slid to her threadbare, outdated coat and the cheap, plastic-looking pocketbook on the seat beside her. Money. She had none, or very little. And opening businesses took more than education and smarts. It took money.

She tilted her head to the side. "Why, um . . . I mean, do you mind if I ask you a personal question?"

"Nope. Go for it."

"Were you kidding about getting married?"

"No."

"Well, I mean . . . it's just that you don't seem very upset."

"Well, it's inconvenient," he confessed. "But no, I'm not upset. I wasn't in love with her."

Eleanora sat back, her eyebrows furrowing, her smile fading. "What?"

"I didn't . . . I mean, we weren't in love with each other. That's the truth."

"Then why were you marrying her?"

"You can marry people for reasons other than love," he said, feeling a little defensive.

"Like what?"

"Like . . . I'm about to lose my inheritance." She stared at him, her face expressionless, her eyes rapt. "My grandfather, he's, well, he's a control freak, in addition to being crazy and old-fashioned. He has this theory that a good woman makes a man, well, a *good* man. So he promised to cut me off by my thirty-second birthday if I wasn't married to a good woman. And I mean, I've dated a lot of girls, but I just haven't met, you know, *the one*."

She raised her eyebrows. "You believe in *the one*?"

"Everyone believes in the one, whether they admit it or not."

"Go on."

In for a penny, in for a pound. He might as well tell her everything. "Diantha is an old friend. She agreed to marry me before I turned thirty-two so that I could secure my inheritance. Our plan was to get a quiet divorce this summer."

"Huh," she said, taking another sip of wine. "When's your birthday?"

"Tuesday."

"Four-days-from-now Tuesday?"

"That's the one."

"You were born on Christmas Eve," she said.

He nodded, pouring himself another glass of wine.

"What was her cut?" asked Eleanora.

It was the last thing he expected her to ask. "Wh-what?"

"I assume you were cutting her in? Since your—" She cleared her throat. "—your *marriage* was little more than a business transaction?"

"Yeah. Okay." He chuckled softly, nodding at her with grudging admiration for her candor. "Yeah. I was cutting her in. I would get fourteen million. I promised her one. Not that it matters now because—"

"One million dollars."

"Yeah, but she didn't—"

"One million *dollars*," she repeated.

He nodded. "Yep. But—"

"I'll do it."

Tom's head jerked back as he stared at her in shock. "What? You'll do what?"

"*I'll* marry you for a million dollars."

Laughter bubbled up inside him, and he let it rip for several seconds until he realized she wasn't joking. She was staring at him unblinkingly, her hands folded on the table as if they were working out a business deal at a conference room table.

"You're serious."

"I don't joke about money."

He chuckled, this time nervously. When she didn't join him, his grin faded. She was completely serious.

"I don't think you understand. It was an arrangement, and yes, I was giving her a portion of my inheritance, but Diantha was actually planning to *marry* me. Our families have known one another for ages, and we'd been friends since grade school. Everyone believed that we'd started dating last summer and fallen in love. It took some planning, you know?"

She didn't say a word, just stared back at him, her eyes owllike in their intensity.

"I don't even know you. My family doesn't know you. We just met twenty minutes ago." He tried to keep his voice gentle because he really didn't want to hurt her feelings. "I just don't think it would work."

"You don't think I could pull it off," said Eleanora candidly.

Tom shifted in his seat, placing his arm along the back of the booth between them and facing her.

Her blonde hair was natural, and her face was pretty. He didn't know if she'd had braces or just been blessed with good teeth, but he suspected the latter. She was trim and bright and interesting, but . . .

His eyes slipped to the collar of her uniform, then to her chewed-up nails, and finally to her white tights and sneakers.

She was a "breakfast-all-day" waitress from Colorado, not a viable contender for the wife of Thomas Andrews English. She wouldn't last a minute in Main Line society, and more importantly, his grandfather would see right through her.

As his gaze skated up to her face, he found her eyes glistening, but she lifted her chin proudly. "Forget it. It's a completely ridiculous idea. I . . . I'm going to go."

She started sliding around the booth to escape him, but that strange feeling of desperation encroached again, and Tom stood up quickly to move around the table and block her way. He squatted down, looking up at her. "Wait. Just . . . please. This got weird so fast. We can still talk and there's wine and—"

She swallowed, shaking her head and pulling her coat more snugly around her. "No, thanks. I feel really foolish. It was an absurd suggestion."

"Not absurd, just . . . unrealistic. No one will buy it. They all believed I was in love with Di. They all know I was just stood up by her."

"I get it," she whispered, still looking down at her lap. "Please let me go now."

"What would you do with it?" he asked softly. "The million?"

She relaxed a little, lifting her eyes to his. "I'd buy Evie a nice little apartment here so that she'd feel secure and stop—well, you know—hooking up with random men. And then I'd go to college somewhere like Princeton. Like you and Brooke Shields."

"And then?"

"I'd buy a business . . . or start my own."

"What kind?"

"I don't know. I know how to waitress, so maybe a restaurant. Although what I'd really love is a bookstore. Or a chain of bookstores maybe. And also . . ." Her voice took on a slight edge, and she averted her eyes. "I'd knock down the library in my hometown and have another one built. A good one. A better one."

Because it saved you. The thought tiptoed across his mind, and he knew, in his gut, it was true.

He knew what Diantha had planned to do with the money: she would have financed a new wardrobe, bought a convertible Ferrari, and rented a villa in Monaco for a year. But Eleanora? She'd buy herself a whole new life. A better life. And suddenly, more than his own inheritance, more than anything else on earth, Tom wanted her to have that chance.

"We'd have to go to Vegas," he said quickly before he could rethink it.

Her neck whipped up, her eyes wide and surprised as she searched his face.

"Vegas?"

"There's nowhere else we could get married so quickly."

Her lips wobbled, but she kept them from turning up.

"Vegas," she murmured.

He nodded. "Tonight. So we could be married tomorrow. That would at least give us the weekend to get to know each other."

She tilted her head to the side and finally let her lips spread into a smile. "Are you serious?"

"Are you?"

"You think we can pull it off?"

No. "I have no clue." He shrugged, grinning at her like a stupid fool. "Want to give it a try?"

"I . . ." Her shoulders trembled, and she giggled, still staring up at him. "You're a decade older than I am."

"I don't care if you don't."

"You're rich and classy, and I'm . . . a waitress."

"I think you're more than that."

"I've never been outside of Colorado."

"Maybe it's time to broaden your horizons."

"You're really serious," she breathed.

"Think of it as an adventure." He stared into her eyes, prying one of the hands on her lap into his and weaving their fingers together. "Eleanora Watters, will you marry me for a little while?"

She beamed at him, nodding slowly at first and then faster and faster, her slim fingers gripping his tightly as her cheeks turned pink and her eyes sparkled like a million white lights at Christmastime. "Why not?"

Chapter 3

As the private plane left the tiny Vail airport, headed for Las Vegas, Eleanora trembled with fear and misgivings. Fear because she'd never been on an airplane before; misgivings because she was headed to Las Vegas to marry a complete and total stranger.

Sitting beside Eve Marie, she closed her eyes and tried to take a few deep, calming breaths, but her cousin wouldn't shut up.

"I mean, look at this plane! It's, like, the most beautiful place I've ever been in my whole life, and that lady gave us champagne, Ellie. *Champagne*! The real stuff. Can you believe it?" She lowered her voice a little. "Are you crazy? Or drunk? Please tell me you're drunk. Why are you *marrying* him? It's not like you're pregnant! Are you? No, that's impossible. Oh my God, these seats. They're real leather, Ellie. *Real leather*. Do you know how much this plane probably costs? I don't. Are you going to *sleep* with him? What if he's bad in bed? Then you're stuck with him for life. Maybe you should have tested the goods first. Sweet Jesus, are those *Godivas*?"

The stewardess held out a gold box filled with delicate-looking chocolates, and Evie took four. Eleanora's stomach, which wouldn't stop flipping over, forced her to decline.

She'd already told Evie three times—once when she and Tom interrupted Evie and Van in Van's hotel room, again while they packed their suitcases in the small, shared bedroom of their apartment, and again right before liftoff—that while she was marrying Tom, she wasn't really *marrying* him. It was a temporary marriage; it was just an agreement, an agreement of convenience, the outcome of which would hopefully change Eleanora's life for the better.

Was she going to sleep with him? *No.*

She straightened her neck and looked over the seat in front of her, catching a quick glimpse of Tom, who sat across from Van, staring out the window. His blond hair tumbled over his forehead, and he rubbed his chin with his index finger as Van flirted shamelessly with the stewardess.

Absolutely not.

Although, in fairness, she was positive he wouldn't be bad in bed.

And with that thought, hidden muscles deep inside her body flexed and held, telling her they wouldn't mind finding out.

He was handsome. Sinfully handsome. But Eleanora had met many handsome men since she and Evie moved to Vail. What set Tom English apart was the way he'd looked at her when he said, "We'd have to go to Vegas"—like he was willing to take a chance on her, like she was somehow *worth* the chance he was taking.

Eleanora's mother had run out on them when she was five, and her father, who was a functioning alcoholic, had done his best with four kids, but there was very little time left for little Eleanora, who always had her nose in a book anyway. She'd only heard from him twice since leaving home three years ago with Eve Marie, who'd actually been their reason for leaving: her new stepfather was paying the sixteen-year-old way too much unwanted attention, and Eve Marie had confessed her fears to Eleanora. They'd hitchhiked to Vail, lied about Eve Marie's age, found jobs as waitresses at Auntie Rose's and used Eleanora's meager savings for a shabby one-bedroom apartment.

Enrolling herself in college courses had taken courage, but Eleanora had read enough books to know that the best way out of poverty was an education, and though she knew she'd likely be in her late thirties before her dreams took shape, at least she *had* dreams, and at least she was trying to make them come true.

And then Tom English had walked into her life, and suddenly she had the chance to fast-track her dreams.

She peeked over the seat again, and he looked up just in time to catch her eyes, locking his with hers. His mustache twitched a little as his lips quirked into a grin, and Eleanora's heart took off at a gallop, her own smile answering his. He lifted his champagne glass and toasted her, his gaze never leaving hers as he tilted his head back and let the champagne bubbles slide down his throat. Suppressing a whimper, Eleanora hunched down, turning to Evie, who was still rhapsodizing and scolding her older cousin in an unbridled stream of scattered, enthusiastic thought.

Tom chuckled softly, watching her blonde head disappear back behind the seat.

She reminded him a little of a gopher, looking over at him with those wide, liquid eyes before ducking back down.

"You think your gramps is going to buy this?" asked Van, checking out the stewardess's ass as she headed back to the galley.

"I don't know," answered Tom honestly. "Can't hurt to try, though. What's the worst he can do?"

"Disown you," said Van.

"Like I said, can't hurt to try."

Van's eyes were uncharacteristically serious when he asked, "What if she tries to get her hooks in you?"

"Who? Eleanora?"

"Yeah."

Not that Tom would necessarily mind having her hooks in him right this minute, but he appreciated that Van's question was sensible. "We'll have to sign something in Vegas. Something about her getting a million and me getting a divorce."

"I'll draw it up," said Van, who rarely used his law degree, though it certainly came in handy at times. "She's cute. I'll give you that. Maybe you can sample the goodies before you say sayonara."

Van turned to the window and closed his eyes while Tom straightened up to get another look at Eleanora. Cute? Nah. She was stunning. She was the hottest girl he'd ever seen. He stared at her blonde head unobserved, and a thought took over his brain: temporary nuptials or not, she deserved a nice, decent wedding. Not some five-dollar cheesefest at an Elvis chapel, but something decent, something she could remember fondly after they'd gotten their money and said their good-byes.

Taking a notebook out of the briefcase he'd stowed under the seat in front of him, he started a list that he didn't complete until they began their descent into Las Vegas.

"I'm sure you'll have everything you need," said Tom, grinning at Eleanora as he walked the cousins to their room at the Imperial Palace, the newest and best hotel on the Strip. "But if you don't, just call downstairs. They'll charge anything you need to me."

Not knowing what she could possibly need, she nodded at him, chancing a glance behind her to find Evie and Van making out in the hallway a ways back. She paused at her hotel room door, holding the key in her hand and turning around to look at Tom.

"Why are you doing this?"

He shrugged. "I was fairly certain that my inheritance was a lost cause. You made me wonder if I shouldn't give it one last chance."

Guilt embraced her. As much as Tom English's million dollars would help her start a whole new life, she felt mercenary taking his money for something as simple as saying "I do" once or twice at a sham wedding. Perhaps he had plans for the fifteen million. "Do you need it? The money?"

"Not really, I guess. I have a good education. I work with my father at my grandfather's financial firm, English & Son, but I could find another job at a different bank if I needed to." He flattened his hand against the wall by her door, caging her on two sides, and she fought the impulse to step into him. "But life will be easier with the money. More doors will stay open to me if I stay on at my family's firm. And . . ."

His eyes flickered as they stared into hers.

"And . . . ?"

Did his cheeks flush a little, or was that her imagination?

He shrugged again. "I like it that you'll be able to chase your dream sooner than later. Buy your bookstores. Build a library. Go to Princeton. I could help you with that, you know." His grin brightened his whole face. "Funny thing, my great-great grandfather built the library there. Just say the word, and I'll make a few calls."

Her eyes had watered as he confessed that he wanted to help her. She wasn't the type of girl who'd had much help in life—no lucky breaks, no windfalls, no happy twists of fate. Not until Tom English had walked into her life.

And suddenly she heard herself whisper, "You're something between a dream and a miracle."

His eyes—his warm, kind eyes—widened suddenly, heating up and darkening as he took a step toward her.

"E-Elizabeth Barrett Browning wrote that," she said quickly. "I didn't make that up. I borrowed it."

"Barrett," said Tom, reaching out to touch her cheek with his fingertips, the touch as soft as breath. "Not Burnett."

Leaning into his touch, she looked into his eyes and grinned curiously, uncertain of his meaning.

"Your cousin said 'Burnett' this morning," he explained, grinning back at her.

"Oh," she whispered, chuckling softly. "Yes. *Barrett*."

His thumb swiped gently over her bottom lip, and Eleanora's breath caught. She wondered if he'd dip his head and kiss her. She hoped he would. Oh God, had she ever wanted anything more?

"*You're* the dream," he said softly, staring deeply into her eyes.

"Tom . . ." she sighed, taking another step toward him, the front of her sweater grazing the nubby, tan corduroy of his jacket.

Suddenly he shook his head like he was coming out of a trance and took a step back, dropping his hand. She watched him fist it by his side, then flex his fingers, spreading them as though in punishment.

"I'll see you tomorrow," he muttered.

Then he turned and walked away.

His name lingered on the tip of her tongue as she watched him stalk away, his legs long in dark jeans, his shoulders hunched forward. As he passed Van and Evie, he stopped and whispered something by Van's ear that caused his friend to break away from Evie, give her a quick hug, and follow Tom down the hall toward the elevator. Eleanora watched until they were out of sight, then shifted her gaze to Evie.

"Someone's in a pissy mood," her cousin observed, hurrying down the hall. "I guess you didn't invite him in, huh?"

I would have, thought Eleanora, steadying her trembling fingers and working the key into the lock. "I think he was . . . just tired. Or something."

"Or something, all right. He practically growled at Van to join him for a drink downstairs."

Eleanora twisted the key and reached down for her suitcase, pushing the door open and feeling along the wall for a light switch. Evie tumbled into the room behind her, knocking into Eleanora, who was frozen in place.

Floor-to-ceiling windows looked out on the Strip, and because of the mirrors on the walls and ceilings, it gave the illusion that the room was decorated in twinkle lights. It was like being inside a jewelry box, she thought, sighing in appreciation. She stepped down two carpeted stairs into the large bedroom suite, which held two queen-size beds, a sofa, and a table with two chairs, not stopping until her fingers gingerly touched the massive plates of glass.

"Wow!"

Eleanora looked over her shoulder at Evie, whose mouth gaped in wonder.

"Oh, Ellie!" said Evie, approaching the first of two beds, then looking up at Eleanora with a beaming smile. "Look!"

Draped across the bed was a white gown covered in clear dry-cleaning plastic.

"It's a wedding dress! Try it on, Ellie!"

Eleanora crossed the room slowly, her eyes glued to the beautiful dress. She carefully slid the plastic up and lifted the hanger from the bed. The dress was strapless and calf length, made entirely of white lace, except for a pale-blue sash around the waist. It was, hands down, the most beautiful dress Eleanora had ever seen.

"There's a card!"

Evie picked up a white envelope from the bedspread and held it out to her cousin.

With trembling hands, Eleanora opened the envelope and read aloud, "Every bride deserves a wedding dress. Thank you for marrying me tomorrow. Tom."

Evie fell back on the other bed, hands pressed over her heart, sighing dramatically. "I wish I'd gone for him! He's utterly dreamy, Ellie!"

Just then, the doorbell rang, and Evie leaped up. Hoping it was Tom, come back to kiss her good-night, Eleanora rushed to the stairs, only to find a bellhop wheeling in a table covered with a white tablecloth. On it, there was a silver ice bucket with a bottle of champagne, two glasses, and a platter of chocolate-covered strawberries.

"Here, miss?" asked the young man, carrying the table down the two stairs and wheeling it beside the windows.

"F-fine," stammered Eleanora, holding Tom's card to her breasts as she watched the bellhop slide the chairs from the room table to the linen-covered table.

"He asked me to say, 'Welcome to Las Vegas, Watters cousins. If there's anything you need, the Imperial—and Tom English—are at your command.'" He grinned at them, eyebrows raised, and Eleanora realized that he was waiting for instruction.

"Um. Oh, well . . . thank you. We're fine. We're great. N-no commands just now."

"Very good. Enjoy!"

He sped toward the door, opened and closed it, leaving the girls alone.

Evie turned around in slow motion to face Eleanora, her eyes wide as saucers, then started jumping up and down and clapping, racing over to the table by the windows and begging to pop the cork.

Caught up in the excitement of the moment, Eleanora shrugged and giggled, "Go ahead!" and a moment later the cork flew across the room. And the unlucky Watters cousins were suddenly the luckiest girls in the world, sitting on top of Las Vegas, sampling chocolate-covered strawberries for the first time in their lives, and marveling at the kindness of Eleanora's temporary intended.

Chapter 4

Tom left a message that Eleanora and Evie were to meet him and Van in the lobby at one o'clock the next afternoon. First, they needed to go to the Regional Justice Center to secure a marriage license, and then they could head to the Wee Kirk o'the Heather Wedding Chapel, which Tom had reserved for a three o'clock ceremony. A busy afternoon.

And frankly, Tom would have been looking forward to seeing her again if his head wasn't pounding like someone kept swinging at his skull with a sledgehammer. Slumped in a lobby chair, he couldn't remember the last time he'd drunk so damn much or felt so completely awful the next day. At least Van didn't look much better.

"I should have said no to the second bottle," griped Van, his head resting on the back of a low, brightly colored floral chair. "But you were so pissed off, and the first bottle made you so much more . . . pleasant."

Tom groaned, staring up at the ceiling, where a multifaceted crystal chandelier made his head ache even worse. He fished his sunglasses from the pocket of his short-sleeved, white dress shirt and put them on. Better. Not much, but better.

"And why the hell I made that promise to keep you from knocking on her door, I'll never know, but you owe me your firstborn as payment. I have bruises all over my body from keeping you off the tenth floor last night. I think I missed my calling as a linebacker."

Tom winced, wishing it wasn't true, but it was.

He didn't remember much from last night, but he definitely remembered Van physically sitting on him to keep him from waking up Eleanora to "get to know her better."

"Sorry," he rasped. "I'll make it up to you."

"Have I mentioned that I think this whole thing is a risky, shitty idea?"

"Yeah," muttered Tom. "Multiple times."

"I'm not even sure a notarized prenup will hold up in court. It hasn't been filed."

"Doesn't matter," said Tom. "I'm still doing it."

"I hope you at least get fucked," said Van, quickly adding, "you know, in the good way."

"Shut up, Van."

Van leaned back in his chair again and sighed loudly to mark his disapproval. He needn't have bothered. Tom already knew that he was in trouble.

It was bad enough that he was marrying a complete stranger. On top of it, he was wildly attracted to his temporary child-bride, and now, in some warped, pathetic, predictable, cautionary-tale twist of fate, he'd actually started falling for her too. Somewhere between watching her tell off that asswipe at Auntie Rose's, swapping favorite books, drinking Asti Spumante, and ending up in Vegas, thirty-one-year-old Tom English had let twenty-two-year-old Eleanora Watters get under his skin.

He scrunched his eyes shut under his sunglasses and shook his head. It was so clichéd, it made his stomach flip over with disgust, and yet . . . there it was, deep in his gut: he liked her. He liked her more than he'd ever liked, well, anyone.

Not that it mattered.

Because today was just a means to an end: get married, secure his inheritance, and get a divorce. He wasn't interested in messing up her plan to go to college and open a business, and fuck knew she wasn't an appropriate choice, on any level, for the wife of Tom English. Aside from the gaping decade age difference between them, they were incompatible in every possible way, right? Right.

But while such clearheaded thinking should have squelched Tom's infatuation, it didn't. He felt like a lovesick teenager when he remembered the way she'd looked at him when she murmured, "You're something between a dream and a miracle." His heart had doubled in size as he stared down at her face, stroking her soft, twenty-something skin, while his mind had fantasized about every filthy thing he'd like to do to her in bed.

Damn it.

He'd been so furious with himself, he'd grabbed Van and made his friend help him polish off a bottle of Dewar's before ordering another.

Fuck.

"Tom?"

And fuck again.

Because he would have known her voice anywhere, and he was reminded of a line from *Romeo and Juliet*: "My ears have not yet drunk a hundred words of that tongue's utterance, yet I know the sound: Art thou not Romeo and a Montague?"

Nope. She's Eleanora. And almost an English.

He opened his eyes, and they instantly widened, his fingers moving to the stem by his ear to pull his glasses off his face. His head stopped aching as he rose slowly to his feet, never taking his eyes off her.

If he was a goner before, now he had one foot in the grave.

She was stunning. She was heartbreakingly, mind-bendingly, gorgeously, stupendously beautiful.

"You got the dress," he murmured.

"I love it," she answered, grinning up at him, her face a mix of pleasure and shyness.

She'd curled her long, blonde hair into soft waves that fell past her shoulders, pinned over one ear and secured with a white blossom. Her skin was luminous, and her eyelashes were dark and long, framing the loveliest blue eyes he'd ever seen. Dropping his gaze to her lips, he felt his body tighten in response to the glossy, pink pillows he found there. He stared at her as they formed his name.

"Tom?" she prompted.

He cleared his throat and jerked his eyes to hers. "Yeah, uh, the dress looks . . . I mean, I'm glad it fits. You look . . ." He may as well be honest with her. His voice dropped lower and sounded gravelly in his ears. ". . . *stunning*."

"Told you, Ellie," said Eve Marie from behind her, nudging her cousin's arm with a simple bouquet of calla lilies and looking up at Tom. "We charged the flowers to you."

"That's fine."

Van finally stood up, huffing loudly to draw Tom's attention.

"Last chance," he mouthed over the cousins' heads.

Tom looked back down at Eleanora's expectant face.

Too late.

The chapel Tom had reserved wasn't at all what Eleanora had expected for her impromptu Vegas wedding. Honestly, she had cringed inside at the thought of an Elvis impersonator officiating—but then, Tom was surprising her at every turn. The Wee Kirk o'the Heather Wedding Chapel, though situated beside a gas station on the Strip, was surprisingly traditional inside.

Once they arrived via limo, Eleanora was quickly whisked away by a wedding coordinator, while Tom, Eve Marie, and Van were shown into the chapel. She waited in the vestibule just outside the sanctuary, her hands sweating around the bouquet of flowers Evie had ordered, her breathing quick and choppy.

Even though he barely knew her, Tom had done everything possible to make today special for her, and Eleanora couldn't help but be deeply touched by his kindness.

Unlike other little girls who dreamed about the man they'd eventually marry at their perfect fairy-tale wedding, Eleanora Watters hadn't indulged in such fantasies. All three of her older siblings had children, but none was married, and while Eleanora had attended the weddings of Evie's mother to her second and third husbands, she didn't have any fond memories of the events.

Most of Eleanora's ideas about love and weddings came from the books she'd read and the movies she'd watched, though she was enough of a realist to separate fact from fiction and recognize that such fanciful notions would probably never apply to her and her life.

And yet . . .

Here was Tom English, the very epitome of a rich, handsome, fairy-tale prince, treating her with kindness, looking at her with those hot, dark eyes, and touching her face like she was, somehow, already precious to him.

"Are we ready, dear?"

Eleanora nodded at the wedding coordinator, and the older woman knocked twice on the closed double doors in front of them. Instantly, the wedding march sounded from inside the chapel, the doors magically opened, and Eleanora walked down the aisle toward Tom.

If he'd thought her beautiful in the lobby of the Imperial Palace, here, in a tiny Vegas chapel, walking toward him in white with a sweet smile, she looked almost angelic.

She handed her bouquet to Eve Marie, and Tom raised his hands so she could take them, her small fingers threading effortlessly through his.

"You sure you want to do this?" he whispered once the music ended.

Her smile grew a little bigger, and she nodded at him, giving him the same words she'd said when she accepted his proposal. "Why not?"

"Okay," he said, grinning back at her before turning to the officiant. "I guess we're ready."

He'd paid for the basic wedding package. No Elvis. No silliness. No cheesy tomfoolery. Just the vows necessary to pronounce them husband and wife, and a dozen posed photos after the service. Why he'd sprung for the photos, he wasn't sure—he'd checked the box before giving it a lot of thought. She could throw them away later if she didn't want them.

"Then let's begin."

Tom nodded, then looked back at Eleanora, whose fingers tightened around his as the older gentleman started speaking.

"Friends, we are gathered here today to join Thomas English and Eleanora Watters in marriage. At Tom's request, I will begin this ceremony with some words by Elizabeth Barrett Browning."

Eleanora's eyes widened for a just a moment before she tilted her head to the side, smiling up at him with wonder.

The officiant read in a clear voice, "An excerpt from a letter to Robert Browning, from his wife, Elizabeth: *You cannot*

*guess what you are to me—you cannot—it is not possible:—
and though I have said* that *before, I must say it again . . .
for it comes again to be said. It is something to me between
dream and miracle, all of it—as if some dream of my earliest
brightest dreaming-time had been lying through these dark
years to steep in the sunshine, returning to me in a double
light.* Can *it be, I say to myself, that* you *feel for me* so? *can
it be meant for me? . . . Could it be that heart and life were
devastated to make room for you?"*

"*They leave the ground fallow before the wheat,*" she murmured, her intelligent eyes glistening and yet somehow
severe as she stared up at him. "How in the world did you—"

"It doesn't matter," he whispered, his heart throbbing
with tenderness for her.

It had taken the hotel concierge hours and hours—and
a couple hundred dollars—working with a lady at the Las
Vegas Public Library this morning, to track down the source
of the words Eleanora had whispered to Tom last night.
But it was worth it. Looking into her eyes now, he decided
that every second he'd waited, every cent he'd spent on the
search, had been worth it to ensure that she was married to
him with a few words that actually meant something to her.

"It matters," she answered softly, her voice breaking a little even as she managed a smile for him.

"Thomas English," intoned the officiant, "repeat after
me."

Tom stared into Eleanora's eyes as he repeated the vows,
promising to love, honor, and cherish her. And he'd be lying
if he said his own eyes didn't burn a little as she returned
the words, her expression bright and confident as her lips
moved softly to form the words that bound her life to his.

"And now, by the authority vested in me by the state of
Nevada, I pronounce you man and wife. Mr. English, you
may kiss your bride."

It hadn't occurred to Tom that he'd be given permission to kiss Eleanora, that it would be expected. After last night, he'd sort of made a deal with himself that he wouldn't touch her, knowing that if he did, his feelings for her would tumble into an emotional abyss, and he strongly doubted he'd ever be in possession or control of them again.

She must have seen the fear cross his face, because her expression cooled as she straightened her spine and lifted her chin. "You don't have to."

Did she think he didn't *want* to? Could she possibly believe—even for a second—there was a universe in which he *didn't* want to feel the softness of her lips beneath his? It wasn't okay with him for her to believe that . . . because it simply wasn't true.

"I *want* to."

Releasing her hands, he palmed her cheeks, gently urging her closer. Eleanora took a step toward him, closing the distance between them, the fitted lace of her bodice flush against the crisp, white cotton of his shirt.

Tom bent his neck, closing his eyes as he leaned toward her, feeling her fingers wrap around his forearm and tighten as his lips alighted on hers. She gasped softly as they made contact, stealing his breath as surely as she was stealing his heart. Her breasts pushed against his chest as she surged forward, arching into him, and he flicked his tongue along the seam of her lips to see if she would open to him. When she did, he tilted his head to the side, lowering his hands to her waist so he could gather her into his arms.

His toes curled in his shoes. His blood sluiced to his groin, where it pooled, hot and demanding, making him hard and needy for her—for this woman who could now legally call herself Mrs. Thomas English.

Eleanora English. His wife.

His brain stuttered over the words, and he drew back from her, breathless and panting, as he looked into her eyes. They were almost black, lazy and drugged as they opened, her body straining into his with every ragged breath she took. Her hands had wrapped around his neck at some point, her fingers braided together on the back of his throat.

And it all felt like heaven.

But it's an arrangement, his head insisted. *It's only an arrangement, and it's temporary.*

The stab of pain he felt in the vicinity of his heart made him wince, and he dropped his arms slowly, waiting for her to untangle her fingers before he took a step away from her.

"Tom," she murmured, her eyes soft and searching.

"Thank you for marrying me," he said, taking her hand and leading her out of the chapel.

Chapter 5

It was almost four o'clock by the time they'd signed the marriage certificate and taken their photos, but all Eleanora really wanted, especially after that kiss, was to spend some time alone with her new husband.

Oh, she knew that their marriage was temporary. She knew that tomorrow they'd fly to Philadelphia, she'd meet his grandfather on Tuesday, and regardless of the outcome of that meeting, they'd say farewell soon after.

But for one brief, shiny, sparkling moment in her dull, gray life, she was Eleanora Watters English, and she intended to enjoy it.

Waiting for the limo outside the chapel after the ceremony and photos, Evie snuggled against Van and grinned at her cousin. "Well, you did it. You're, like, *married*, Ellie!"

Glancing down at her thin, gold wedding band, Eleanora looked over her shoulder at Tom, who stood behind her. "I guess I am."

Van stuck out his hand, adding solemnly—his words clearly meant more for Tom than for her—"I hope you don't regret it."

Eleanora took Van's hand and shook it. "You don't need to worry. We have an agreement. I intend to honor it."

Van nodded, but Eleanora was surprised to feel Tom's hands land on her hips, pulling her back against his body.

During the pictures, he'd followed the directions of the photographer, putting his arm around her shoulders or pressing his lips to her cheek, but this was the first time he'd reached for her since they'd kissed in the chapel.

"Let's not worry about that right now," he murmured near her ear, his hot breath making shivers skate down her back as he wrapped his arms around her, resting them under her breasts. "Let's just enjoy Vegas."

"What did you have in mind?" asked Evie, smiling at Tom over Eleanora's shoulder.

Tom spoke close to Eleanora's ear again. "Any chance you like Donny and Marie?"

Evie gasped so loud, her cousin couldn't help but chuckle. "Well, even if I don't, I know someone who does."

"Did he say *Donny and Marie*? As in . . . *Osmond*?" Evie squealed.

Tom laughed, holding on to Eleanora a little tighter.

"Aw, honey," griped Van, "I wanted to *show you my room*."

"And I would love to *see your room*," said Evie, "but the man just mentioned Donny Osmond!"

Tom spun Eleanora in his arms, and suddenly she found herself looking up into his deep, blue eyes, which were crinkled and merry, to match his smile.

"So? Want to go to their show tonight?"

"Did you really get tickets?"

He nodded, grinning at her like the cat who got the cream. "It's their Christmas special. It's going to be televised."

"Ellie! Ellie! Ellie! *Say yes!*" yelled Evie from behind her.

Eleanora beamed at Tom. "I'd love to go."

"You're wrecking my plans," muttered Van, giving Tom a dirty look as the limo pulled up.

Tom pressed a kiss to Eleanora's forehead, and her stomach filled with butterflies, making her feel weak and strong at the same time as she basked in the way she felt special and precious to someone for the first time in her life. "I've read about this. This is *spoiling*, isn't it? You're spoiling me."

"So let me. It's only temporary, right?"

"Right." Her cheeks flushed hot, and she dropped his eyes, wishing she could ignore the sting that accompanied his words. Plastering a smile on her face, she looked up at him again. "Thank you. Donny and Marie it is."

Leading her into the back of the limo, he held her hand as they were driven the two miles back to the Imperial Palace, and the whole way, Van grumbled about the best-laid plans going to hell, with Evie assuring him that he'd have plenty of time to get the best lay after *she* got a chance to see Donny Osmond.

Tom had barely seen the show.

As much as possible, he'd watched his bride, still radiant in white, as she experienced her first live production of . . . anything.

At dinner before the show, Eleanora had shared a little bit about her background: she'd grown up in a tiny town called Romero, three hours south of Vail, where her father worked as a mechanic. He could tell from her reluctance to talk about her childhood that it probably hadn't been very easy or very happy, unlike his, which had been steeped in unfathomable wealth and endless opportunity. She spoke with some guarded affection about her high school English teacher—whom Evie had simultaneously labeled "heinous" and "a spaz"—and mentioned the library, where she'd worked after school and on weekend mornings until she left Romero at nineteen. Neither woman spoke freely about why they'd left their hometown, but Tom sensed that the reason was sound and serious and that the cousins were bound by its necessity. He couldn't help but notice the way Evie looked at her older cousin, with an adoration on the edge of worship, which left little doubt that Eleanora had extricated Evie from something potentially toxic . . . or worse.

Learning more about her added dimension and strength to a woman he admired more by the minute. Despite her young age, she was smart and ambitious, protective and brave, all wrapped up in the body of a goddess, with the face of an angel. And she was his wife. The words circled in his mind as he watched her: *This goddess–angel is my wife. In the eyes of the law, she belongs to me, and I belong to her.*

After dinner, they walked over to the Flamingo, where they took their third-row VIP seats for the televised show. Eleanora suddenly grasped Tom's hand, her cheeks pink and lips glossy as she faced him.

"Thank you for this," she said, her smile dazzling. "For everything. For the best Christmas ever."

"It's not even Christmas yet," he responded, feeling shaky and adolescent, his feelings for her taking his head, his heart, his very soul, by storm.

"See what I mean?" she joked, facing the stage and entwining her fingers with his before shifting their bound hands to her lap.

He didn't want to freak her out by staring at her, but at every possible opportunity—when there was a gag they could laugh at, after every song as he held her hand and didn't clap, and sometimes during an especially poignant Christmas carol—he'd glance over at her. She sat up straight, her posture perfect, her chin high. Her strong cheekbones made apples of her cheeks when she smiled or giggled, which made her look younger and softer than twenty-two, and he wondered what it would be like to always see her smiling, to never again see the lines of worried caution that crossed her face with too much regularity. Her hand was warm and small in his, her fingers elegant and soft threaded between his, and when he wasn't looking at her, he was concentrating on the feeling of her skin pressed against his and wondering what he wouldn't give for the right to hold her hand like this forever.

What was happening to him? And why now? And why so fast? And why, for heaven's sake, with her?

He'd had his pick of girls at the country club, at Princeton, in Philadelphia society. What was it about *this* girl—down-on-her-luck Eleanora Watters—that so pulled at his heartstrings? She was beautiful, yes, but it was so much more than that. It was the heart of a lion inside the body of a lamb. It was a poet's soul in a waitress's dress. It was a girl who deserved so much more than getting a shitty hand in life. And it was her sitting beside him now, watching the whole world with wonder at Christmastime, when the show was just some forgettable Vegas tripe. She was unspoiled and honest, unentitled and hardworking, hopeful when she had every right to be bitter. She was magnificent. How in the hell could he *not* fall for her?

Once the curtain was down and the lights up, Evie and Van hurried back to the hotel, but Tom and Eleanora strolled hand in hand, walking leisurely under the bright, neon lights of the Strip.

"Did you like it?" he asked her after a while.

"I loved it."

"It's different being there in person, isn't it? Did you think it would be the same as watching it on TV?"

She took a deep breath and exhaled slowly. "I don't know how to explain this, but I don't have thoughts like that at all. If you'd asked me yesterday my thoughts on seeing Donny and Marie on TV versus seeing them live, I wouldn't have been able to answer you. I wouldn't have had an inkling of what it was like to see movie stars singing and dancing ten feet away from my eyes. I would have wondered if you were making fun of me."

"And maybe dressed me down with your numbers routine?"

She whipped her head to his, a slow smile spreading across her face. "You caught that yesterday morning, huh?"

"I don't think anyone at the restaurant missed it." He squeezed her hand. "You were brilliant."

She sighed. "I get sick of it, you know?"

"Getting hit on?"

"Getting hit on, being objectified . . . the assumption that I'm so desperate, I'm a sure thing."

"I don't see you like that, you know."

She stopped walking, looking up at him, the red, yellow, and green lights above them sparkling in her eyes. "I know."

"What if I kissed you again?" he whispered.

"What if you did?"

"You wouldn't mind?"

"Maybe I'd mind if you didn't."

He dipped his head and caught her bottom lip between his, winding his arms around her slim form and pulling her against his body. She was lithe and small next to him, and she tasted like pineapple juice and rum, and Tom knew that he'd never drink a piña colada for as long as he lived without thinking about Eleanora English.

She whimpered into his mouth, and he swallowed the sound, slipping his tongue between her lips, feeling the ridges of her teeth before her tongue met his. The wet velvet lit his blood on fire, and he gripped her harder, pushing against her lower back to make sure she could feel the ridge of his erection pressed against her stomach, and wondering if it was possible for her to want him half as much as he wanted her.

Their second kiss, in the middle of the Las Vegas Strip with a thousand anonymous witnesses, was far more intimate than the one they'd shared in the tiny chapel in front of an old man and their two closest friends. She could feel the outline of Tom's whole body against hers, and Eleanora arched her back, pressing her breasts against his chest and sighing when he growled her name near her ear. His lips grazed her throat, and she leaned her head back to give him complete access, his arms tightening around her as he pressed hot little kisses to her skin, at her pulse, in the tiny cove at the base of her throat.

A couple of kids snickered as they walked by, one of them saying, "Fuck her, man!" while the other advised them to "Get a room!" and Eleanora remembered herself, placing her palms flat against Tom's chest and pushing gently. He straightened, looking down at her, his eyes dark blue and fierce.

"You're like a drug. The more I touch you, the more of you I want."

I know the feeling, she thought.

But this is only temporary, whispered her heart.

"Tom," she said, pushing against his chest with a little more force as she caught her breath. "We shouldn't."

He loosened his arms and took a step away from her, searching her face, his expression intense, almost furious. "I didn't see you coming. I didn't expect you."

"I didn't expect you either."

"What now?" he asked.

Was he hoping she'd invite him to her room or accept an invitation to his? If she slept with him, she'd know how it felt to have his body slide into hers, claim hers, love hers. She'd know the wonder of tender, loving sex with this man, with her husband. She'd know how it felt to be treasured for a brief, unforgettable moment. But . . .

How, then, could she bear to return to her world? For the rest of her life, she would measure every man against Tom, and none would measure up to her beautiful, thoughtful husband of three days. She'd be ruined for happiness, and though she'd never expected much, now that she'd had a taste, she couldn't deny she wanted more. Wanting it from Tom, however, was not only unrealistic, but unfair. He'd been clear with her. She was a solution to a problem that, once resolved, would conclude their business. And her payment for services rendered was more than fair.

"I haven't seen the pool yet," she said, glancing up at the sky and blinking back the useless tears she wished away. "I bet it's lovely at night."

When she met his eyes, he quickly concealed a grimace with a quick, disingenuous smile. He was disappointed in her suggestion.

"Tom," she said gently, "it's not that I don't want to."

"Then . . . ?"

"We're temporary, and I know that, but you're already in my head. I can't afford to have you in my heart too. And if I gave you my body—even for one night—I know that's where you'd end up: in my heart. And when we shake hands and walk away from each other, you'd take my heart with you. And I'd be left alone without it. I can't live without my heart, Tom." She paused, swallowing over the lump in her throat. "I can't . . . I can't let myself fall for you."

His eyes had grown progressively more stricken as she spoke, as if he understood her words so perfectly, they could have come out of his mouth just as easily.

"I understand," he said, offering her his elbow and a genuine, if sad, smile. "The pool it is."

She placed her hand on his bare arm, and the springy hairs tickled her fingers for a moment until she tightened her grip, letting him lead her around the back of the hotel through well-lit, landscaped pathways.

"Why *The Swiss Family Robinson*?" she asked in an effort to make conversation that would steer them to safer waters.

He chuckled softly, the noise welcome on the warm winter breeze. "I was wondering when you'd ask me about that."

"It's not an obvious choice."

He shrugged. "But it's my favorite. I think it's the main character, the oldest brother, Fritz. He's intelligent and strong, but impetuous. I always liked him."

"No wonder."

"What does that mean?"

"It sounds like you," she said, pushing a long lock of blonde hair behind her ear.

He preened internally from her praise, accepting and savoring it as they walked into the moonlight.

"But isn't it *Fitz*?" she asked. "Like Fitzwilliam?"

"No, *Burnett*," he teased. "It's Fritz with an *r*. A German name for a Swiss family."

"Ah." She sighed, then cocked her head, looking up at him. "But you have to admit that Fitz sounds nicer. Like Fitzwilliam Darcy."

"Mr. Darcy. You're an Austen fan."

"Show me a woman who isn't!"

He laughed again, pulling his arm away from her so that he could find his room key in his pocket and show it to the pool gate attendant. A moment later, they were afforded access to the dark, quiet patio surrounding the glowing, blue pool.

"So why else is it your favorite?" she asked.

"I guess I liked the sense of adventure. The idea of living on a deserted island. And, well, if I'm honest, I loved the idea of four brothers. I grew up alone, and I would—oh, I don't know. I guess I was a little jealous of the Robinsons with all those brothers."

"I didn't know you were an only child."

Tom gestured to a double chaise by the pool's edge, and Eleanora sat down, swinging her legs up on the canvas seat as Tom sat down beside her. "Technically, I'm not. I have a little brother, my father's son from his second marriage. But he's only eighteen. We barely know each other."

"I see," she said, her voice kind and warm. "So lots of brothers sounded ideal."

"A big family sounded ideal," said Tom, putting his arm around her shoulders and pulling her against his side. "Still does."

"Is that what you want someday?"

"Mm-hm," he breathed softly. "A gaggle of kids so they're never lonesome, so they always have each other."

"Sounds nice," she said. "Coming from four, I always thought—well, when I thought of having a family, which wasn't very often—I always imagined it big. I don't know any different."

"A working mom?" he asked. "Managing your bookstores *and* a big family?"

She looked up at him and grinned. "Something like that. Maybe."

He stared into her eyes for a long time, one hand caressing her shoulder as the other reached for her face. Finally, he lowered his lips to hers, kissing her gently, reverently, without the heat from their previous kiss, but with ten times the tenderness.

"I hope you get everything you want," he whispered, his breath soft against her lips. "I like you so much, Eleanora English."

"I like you too," she answered, nestling against his chest and closing her tired eyes.

In no time at all, they were asleep, held fast in each other's arms, their dreams mingling and marrying under the fathomless desert sky.

Chapter 6

When their small plane touched down in Vail the next morning and Van announced that he was staying to spend Christmas with Eve Marie, Tom wasn't certain who was more shocked—him or Eleanora.

"What are you talking about?" demanded Tom, pulling his friend aside on the tarmac as Eleanora did the same with her cousin.

Van rubbed the back of his neck. "We never . . . I mean, we meant to, you know, *seal the deal* last night, but we fell asleep."

"You . . . *what*? You *fell asleep*?"

Van shrugged, looking sheepish. "She was talking about Donny and Marie and how much she liked them, and . . . I don't know . . . I got to thinking if she liked them so much, I should get us a record player and a couple of their records 'cause we could dance and I bet she'd like that. So the concierge rustled up a few albums and brought them up. And then we were dancing and we had some champagne, and before I knew it, I woke up next to her on the couch. Clothes still on. And the phone was ringing because you and Ellie were already waiting for us downstairs."

"I've never known you to blow a sure thing like this. Should I be worried?" asked Tom, smirking at his friend and vastly enjoying Van's obvious discomfort.

"Nah." Van looked over at Eve Marie, who was gesticulating wildly as she told her cousin a similar, if more enthusiastic, version of the story, and Tom noted how his friend's face softened as he looked at her. "Listen, my folks already left for our ski house in Stratton, and Ellie's going back East with you, so I just thought I may as well, I don't know, keep her company. Stick around for a few more days."

"I didn't know they were spending Christmas in Vermont. I've always loved Stratton," said Tom, giving Van a sly smile. "You could easily jump on a plane and join them, you know."

"I kinda—aw, fuck. You want me to say it? I'll say it. I kinda like her. She's, I don't know, she's sorta dumb and sorta sweet, but she makes me laugh, and when she looks up at me with those big, blue eyes, I just . . ."

Tom shook his head at Van with a mixture of teasing and disbelief. "I never thought I'd see it happen."

"This from the one who got married in Vegas yesterday," muttered Van grumpily. "Which, by the way, I still think is completely nuts."

Tom's grin faded, and his voice held a strong note of warning. "Keep your opinions about Eleanora to yourself, okay? For however long, she's my wife. I need you to respect that."

Van scoffed, looking back over at the girls. "I guess I'm not the only one falling for a Watters cousin, huh?"

Tom shrugged, glancing over at Eleanora, who was hugging Evie tightly. She caught Tom's eyes over her cousin's shoulder and winked at him.

"You're definitely not the only one," said Tom, his gaze locked on his bride.

Tom wrote Eve Marie a check for Eleanora's share of January's rent, and the cousins hugged good-bye, with Eleanora promising she'd be back before New Year's. As they stood side by side on the tarmac, waving at the departing cab, Tom reached for Eleanora's hand, delighting in the way she laced their hands together and looked up at him with a sunny smile.

"I'm glad she won't be alone for Christmas," she said.

"Me too. Ready for Philly?"

"I don't know," she said, cocking her head to the side. "Is Philly ready for me?"

He chuckled, putting his arms around her. "Let's hope so."

She leaned against him, her blue eyes serious and her voice husky when she spoke. "It was nice waking up next to you, Tom."

"Yeah," he said, drawing her closer and brushing his lips against her forehead. "For me too." Though, frankly, he wouldn't have minded waking up beside her naked body in a bed, instead of her clothed one in dew-covered pool chairs.

She rested her cheek on his chest, her voice a little muffled when she spoke. "I know that we only have a few days together, but . . ."

"But what, sunshine?"

She leaned back and looked up at him, seemingly surprised by the endearment, though her grin told him it pleased her too.

"Could we just be happy?" she asked. "Just . . . pretend like we're really married? Like this is our first Christmas as a married couple?"

"We really *are* married, and this really *is* our first Christmas as a married couple."

"I know. But you know what I mean . . . Could we just—"

"You mean, get a tree? Drink eggnog? Take a walk in the snow?"

"Exactly," she said, her voice warming. "Maybe watch a Christmas movie. And I can make dinner for us . . . you know, if you wanted me to."

I want you to. I want all of it just as much as you do.

But real life intruded on his dreams.

"If everything goes according to plan, we'll have to go to my grandparents' house for Christmas."

"Oh."

"However, if I'm disowned, we'll hang out at my apartment, and I'll be glad to eat whatever you make."

"They'll believe us, Tom," she said, drawing back to look into his eyes. "We'll make sure of it."

Her eyes were sharp and serious, her pillowed lips pressed together with earnestness. She was so beautiful, such a capable teammate, he couldn't help himself: he leaned down and pressed his lips to hers.

Her hands had been trapped between them, but she looped them around his neck, pulling his head down, sweeping her tongue into his mouth and bowing her back so that their bodies were flush. Her fingers played with the hair on the back of his neck, massaging and pulling, and his body caught fire with the heat of his longing. He groaned into her mouth as he hardened on command, wanting to feel more of her, know more of her, have more of her.

"Eleanora," he panted near her ear. "What are you doing to me?"

"The same thing you're doing to me," she sighed.

He held her tightly, breathing in the sweet scent of her maple syrup hair and reveling in the feeling of her small body pressed so intimately against his. And then it came to him, in a flash, in a flame, in a burst of realization that made him shudder as she clung breathlessly to him:

Love.

Was this love?

He frowned.

Infatuation? Sure.

But love? Impossible.

Even if what he felt was the zygote of a someday love, he wasn't even comfortable calling it that at this point. He'd only just met her. Christ, he barely knew her.

She sighed in his arms and readjusted her cheek against his shoulder, and his heart throbbed with it again—this deep, spreading, as-yet-unnamed feeling that was multiplying with every moment they spent together—and it felt both terrifying and fucking awesome, and frankly, Tom didn't care if he never felt it with another woman for the rest of his life, as long as he got to feel it with Eleanora forever.

Forever.

And therein lay the problem.

He didn't have forever.

He barely had now.

Tom was quiet on the plane ride East, despite Eleanora's attempts to engage him. He wasn't rude to her, just distracted, and finally she stopped trying, resting her head against the window and falling asleep to the white noise of the engine.

When she woke up, it was dark outside and the plane was still. Tom was squatting in front of her, holding her hands, his face gray in the dim light.

"Tom," she murmured.

"Hey, sleepyhead."

"You're like a dream."

"Or a miracle," he said softly, dropping his lips to her hand and kissing it gently. "We're here."

She took a deep breath and sighed, opening her eyes and pulling her hands away so she could stretch her arms over her head. "How long was I out?"

"Hours. We didn't sleep that well last night, I guess."

"Or the night before," she added, feeling around for her shoes with her socked feet. "I could sleep for a million years."

"It's only seven o'clock here. How about some takeout first? Then sleep?"

"Sounds good."

She held out her hands, and he pulled her drowsy body up from the comfortable airplane seat, leading her down the aisle to the open door and down a small set of stairs. The cold air was jarring, and she shivered, wishing she hadn't packed her coat but worn it instead. On the tarmac was a black town car, and Tom opened her door, letting her get settled before climbing in beside her.

"You're cold," he said, sliding closer to her as the car made its way through the small airport gates and onto the adjacent highway.

"A little," she said, rubbing her freezing hands together.

Tom put his arm around her, drawing her against his side, and she rested her head on his shoulder, sighing with pleasure.

Earlier today, when he'd asked, *What are you doing to me?* she'd felt it deep inside, the way she felt an awesome orgasm gather—only it wasn't her muscles clenching in readiness for release, it was her heart clenching in readiness to let go, or let in, or let loose. She didn't recognize the feeling, but her chest tightened, head swam, and she felt dizzy as he held her, the taste of him still on her lips.

It's love, whispered her heart.

It couldn't be, she thought, her eyes suddenly burning as she tried to concentrate on the even rhythm of Tom's breathing near her ear. *It couldn't be. It can't happen this fast. That would be impossible and . . . disastrous.*

Her heart raced, and she clenched her eyes shut, swallowing over the growing lump in her throat, because Eleanora Watters hadn't had much good luck in her life, and recognizing disaster came easily.

She was falling for Tom English.
God damn it, Eleanora.
What a stupid, ridiculous thing to do.

Too soon, they pulled up in front of Tom's apartment building in downtown Philadelphia.

With the light weight of his wife's head on his shoulder, Tom had fantasized for most of the ride that it was
all real—that he'd fallen in love with Eleanora in Vail, gotten married in Vegas, and here he was, bringing his bride
home to Philadelphia to celebrate Christmas and meet his
family. He smiled at his reflection as he thought about her
and their marriage in those terms, and part of him wished
it was true.

Even though it wasn't.

An arrangement. That's all it was.

But . . . did it have to be?

Maybe, after they'd met with his grandfather the day after
tomorrow, no matter what the verdict, he'd ask her to stay
a little longer. Through New Year's. Maybe she could stay
a few weeks, a month, a year. Hell, the way he felt, maybe
she'd consider staying forever.

Maybe she could attend Drexel or Penn or Bryn Mawr.
She could share his apartment, and he could take care of
her. And all the while, they could get to know each other
better: talk until dawn, hold hands as they took walks and
discussed books, have long dinners together while they
shared their dreams and helped each other make them
come true.

Maybe it didn't have to be an arrangement.

Maybe it didn't have to end.

"Are we here?"

Eleanora had been so quiet on the ride home, Tom wondered if she'd fallen asleep, but her voice was crisp, not
sleepy, so she must have been awake the whole time, thinking, just like him.

"We're here, sunshine."

She lifted her head but turned away from him, and by
the time he'd exited and circled the car to open her door,
she was already standing on the curb looking up at his
building.

"You live here?"

He nodded. "Yep. I own the penthouse apartment."

She whistled low, the way she had when he told her that
he'd gone to Princeton. "Whoa."

He reached for her hand, but she didn't give it to him,
adjusting her purse on her shoulder instead, then walking
through the revolving door and into the lobby.

The town car driver loaded their luggage onto a cart, and
the doorman headed for the service elevator, leaving Tom
and Eleanora alone, waiting for the tenant elevator in the
lobby. And Tom realized that Eleanora hadn't looked him in
the eye since they'd arrived. No teasing grins, no entwined
hands . . . nothing.

"Hey," he said, nudging her with his elbow. "You okay?"

"Sure," she answered quickly, staring at the shiny, brass
elevator door.

The bell rang and the doors parted. She stepped forward,
into a far corner, then turned around, staring at the Persian
carpet beneath her feet. Her jaw was clenched tightly, and
she blinked several times.

What was going on? She looked miserable, and he
couldn't bear it—not if he was the cause or could help with
a solution. He reached forward and pressed the button for
the tenth floor, then stepped back against the railing, beside
her but not touching her.

"Are you worried? About my grandfather? About not getting the money?"

She gulped softly, shaking her head, but she didn't answer him.

"Did I do something?"

She shook her head again, reaching up to swipe at her cheek.

"Jesus, Eleanora, please just tell me what's going on."

The bell rang again to signal that they'd arrived at the tenth floor, and Eleanora marched out of the elevator, then stood still in the quiet hallway. She didn't know where to go, and Tom wasn't telling her until she told him what was wrong.

Gently placing his hands on her shoulders, he turned her around to face him, but she kept her head bent, her eyes cast down.

"Please tell me," he whispered.

"I'm falling for you," she said, so softly, he almost didn't believe he'd heard her correctly until she cleared her throat and said it again. "I'm falling for you."

"That's okay," he said, relief flooding his senses and making him sigh raggedly.

"It's *not* okay," she said, finally raising her glistening eyes to his. "It's not okay to fall for someone so quickly. It doesn't make sense, and it scares me. It's not okay to fall for someone you're leaving in three days. That's a great way to break your own heart. It's not okay to fall for someone who's older and more sophisticated and better educated and just needs a wife so that he can—"

Whatever she'd been expecting, suddenly feeling Tom's arms around her and his lips pressed fiercely to hers wasn't it. But her feelings were so intense and she needed the comfort he offered so badly, she let her purse drop to the floor and wound her arms around his neck. She parted her lips and moaned when his tongue found hers, sucking it, then sliding against it until her panties flooded with the heat of her arousal. Her nipples beaded under her sweater, and she rubbed them against his chest with every breath she took, threading her fingers through his soft, blond hair, tilting her head this way, then that, delighting in the tickle of his mustache, tasting him from every angle, and begging fate to let her stay just a little longer in his arms.

A person's forever is a grain of sand on the beach of eternity.
But I won't be greedy. I won't ask for forever.
I just want a little longer.

"I'm falling for you too," he said, his voice gravelly and breathless as he pressed kisses to the top of her head, sliding his hands up her arms to cup her face with his palms.

When he tilted her head up to look at him, his eyes were midnight blue and fierce. "Can you do me a favor?"

"I'll try."

"Help me get a tree tomorrow and decorate it." He smiled at her so hopefully, it made more tears flood her eyes. "Take a walk with me in the snow, and lie next to me on the couch while we watch a Christmas movie. And on Tuesday, after we meet with my grandfather, promise me we'll talk. We'll make sense of this, Eleanora. We'll figure it out together."

She searched his eyes and saw the emotion there—the tenderness, the warmth, the desire, and concern. And she realized something brand-new: she trusted him.

Sniffling softly, she reached up and dried her eyes before offering him a wobbly smile and nodding. "Okay."

"Yeah?"

She nodded again, letting him take her hand and lead her down the hallway to his apartment. "Okay."

Chapter 7

Tom hoped that Eleanora would sleep in his bed with him, but she opted for the guest room instead, and although he longed for her beside him, he didn't challenge her or make her decision any harder.

The next morning, he woke early, his subconscious aware of someone else in his space, moving around, living. Well, and the smell of coffee, pancakes, and bacon were making his mouth water. Pulling on a pair of old jeans over his boxers and leaving his chest bare, he left his room, rubbing his eyes as he moved in the direction of the warm, delicious smells coming from his barely-ever-used kitchen.

She had her back to him, wearing tight, dark-blue jeans and a light-pink sweatshirt that exposed the creamy skin of her left shoulder and made him wonder if she was wearing a bra, though he quickly deduced she probably wasn't, because he didn't see a strap. His mouth watered again, and this time it had nothing to do with breakfast.

As if sensing his presence, she looked over her shoulder, her lovely face brightening with a smile when she found him staring at her.

Then her eyes dropped to his bare chest.

And slowly, ever so slowly, her smile faded, and her breathing became just a touch more audible. When she raised her eyes, they were dark, and as she tugged her bottom lip between her teeth, he was sure he heard a soft whimper.

Tom stalked across the living room, beelining for her, reveling in her wide-eyed stare and the rapid rise and fall of her untethered breasts. Jesus, was there a more beautiful woman on the face of the earth? Nope. No way. No how.

He stopped about a foot from her, his voice more gravelly than casual when he said, "Morning, sunshine."

"M-morning," she breathed, pressing her palms against her cheeks as she stared up at him.

His lips wobbled beneath his mustache, and he laughed softly. "Want me to put on a shirt?"

"No!" she exclaimed, wincing right after her outburst. "I mean . . . oh God . . . you don't have to. I mean . . ."

He reached out and covered one of the hands on her cheeks. "I'm teasing you."

She cocked her head to the side, sliding her palm out from under his so his hand lay flat against the skin of her face, and she leaned against it, her eyes half-lidded and dreamy. "Good morning, husband."

Tom bent his head forward, kissing his wife, his lips a gentle pressure on hers. She opened for him like a flower, winding her arms around his neck and lacing her fingers against his skin. He pulled her into his arms, tilting his head to seal his lips more perfectly over hers. And frankly, he would have kissed her all day if the bacon behind her hadn't started snapping and complaining.

"It's going to burn," she whispered, her breath hot against his lips.

"Let it."

"That would be a waste," she said, leaning back, her eyes asking for more even though her body had started pulling away.

Compromising, he turned her in his arms, holding her from behind, the back of one bare shoulder scorching the skin of his chest. She reached for a wooden spoon—he had wooden spoons?—and moved the bacon around the frying pan a little bit.

He rested his chin on her shoulder, inhaling the sweet smell of this lovely girl and sighing in contentment.

"I didn't even realize I had food."

"You didn't. But you had the name of a grocery store that delivers on your fridge."

He laughed. "You're industrious."

"You don't know the half of it. I have pancakes keeping warm in the oven too," she said, leaning her head to the side.

Tom turned his face toward her, his lips brushing the soft, hot skin of her throat, kissing her once, twice, feeling goose bumps rise beneath his lips, and he sucked on them gently, puckering his lips, then pulling away to nuzzle her soft skin again.

She moaned deep in her throat as he kissed her neck, the low vibration under his lips making darts of pleasure launch with precision to his groin, which stiffened against her backside.

"I want you," he groaned near her ear, taking the lobe between his teeth and flicking his tongue over the soft pillow of prisoned skin. "I've never wanted anyone as much as I want you."

Her breath caught, but she was silent in his arms, the wooden spoon motionless in her hand. "Tom . . ."

"You want me too, Eleanora. I know it. I can feel it."

"I do." She swallowed before dragging in a ragged breath. "But I'm not my cousin. I don't sleep with men just to . . . get ahead."

"No," he said evenly, frustrated by how much he wanted her. "You marry them."

She stiffened a little. "That sounds mercenary."

He sighed, brushing his lips against the back of her neck. "I don't mean it in a bad way. I needed you. You needed me. I'm older and better educated, but you're smart and resourceful. It levels the playing field between us. It makes me feel like there's nothing you couldn't do. It makes me wonder . . ."

"Makes you wonder what?"

. . . if you could start your life as the daughter of an alcoholic mechanic from a one-horse town in Colorado, and somehow end up the wife of a Philadelphia millionaire. For real. Forever.

"If there's anything you can't do."

She took a deep breath, and he sensed she was sorting through his words. Suddenly, she raised her head and pushed the bacon around the pan, making it snap and sizzle. "Well, I can't make unburned bacon if you don't let go of me and set the table. So . . ."

He kissed her neck, letting her go. "On it."

A few hours later, they struggled down his street, Tom clasping the trunk of a Fraser fir in his gloved hands and Eleanora giggling as she walked backward holding on to the top.

"Human at two o'clock," he said, and she burst into laughter, adjusting her course.

"Now?"

"Stroller at eleven, and behind that, a dog walker at two."

She kept her eyes glued to his, swerving to the left, then right. Turning around and walking forward had occurred to her, but it had also occurred to her that it wouldn't be half as much fun as watching him struggle with the tree *and* keep her from colliding with oncoming traffic.

In the crook of each elbow, she carried oversized plastic bags filled with ornaments, lights, and garlands, and she adjusted one of them to her forearm so it wouldn't swing into her shin.

"Fire hydrant. Three o'clock."

She looked up and burst out laughing again. "It's not going to jump out at me, is it?"

He grinned. "Nope. But I hadn't heard you laugh for at least thirty seconds. I was about to go through withdrawal."

"Flirt," she said, rolling her eyes even as her heart pumped with pleasure.

"I'm not a flirt," he said. "I'm married."

"Poor girl."

"Ha! Lucky girl! I'll have you know I'm a catch."

"Oh really? Besides money, good looks, an excellent education, decent taste in books, a private plane, and a bangin' apartment, what makes *you* a catch?"

His eyes sparkled. "You think I'm good-looking?"

She started giggling and rolled her eyes at him again.

"Well, I think *you're* gorgeous," he said, readjusting his grip on the tree trunk. "Apartment building. Nine o'clock."

She stopped, looking behind her shoulder at Tom's luxury building. The doorman rushed to open the side door, but Eleanora had already stepped into the revolving door, cackling with glee as Tom hurried to pull the tree upright so that all three of them would fit in one small compartment of glass.

When they reached the lobby opening, Eleanora stepped out, but Tom purposely went around with the tree again, making her laugh so hard, her stomach was aching by the time he dragged himself and his prize into the lobby and stood before her.

"You might be a little crazy," he deadpanned.

"Me?" she demanded.

"Yes, you, Mrs. English."

"I'm giddy today," she said, taking a deep breath around her giggles. "I haven't had a—"

Realizing what she was about to say, she stopped talking, and her laughter tapered off until they stood in awkward silence.

"Haven't had a what?" asked Tom quietly, as tall and strong as the tree bundled up beside him.

"I haven't had a Christmas tree since my mom left. Since I was five," she said, meeting his eyes.

She didn't cry. She didn't wince. She didn't look away. She wasn't ashamed of who she was. She wasn't going to apologize for her past. It was her truth, it was honest, and she wanted him to know it.

He stared at her, his eyes blue and careful as they searched hers. Finally, he offered her a small smile and nodded. "Then I guess we better get it upstairs and start decorating, huh?"

Picking up the tree without another word, he carried it to the elevator and pressed the call button, but Eleanora stood there in the middle of his lobby, frozen, processing what had just happened.

He could have felt sorry for her, which she would have hated. He could have felt guilty for all the Christmas trees he'd ever had, and she would have hated that too. He could have asked her to talk more about her awful Christmases, and really, she had no interest in talking about her crappy childhood. He could have looked appalled or dismayed and tried to comfort her, which would have been presumptuous and made her defensive.

Instead, he had accepted her truth without judgment and affirmed who she was now without condemning where she'd been. And if she was in danger of falling for him yesterday, she realized today that the deed was done. Though she dared not give it the name it owned, she knew that whatever happened tomorrow at his grandfather's house, leaving him now would cause damage, wreak havoc, and break her heart. Losing him would hurt for a long time. Maybe forever.

"You coming, or what?" he called from inside the elevator.

She turned and ran across the lobby, not stopping until she collided with him, her cold hands reaching for his face and pulling it down to hers. He fumbled to press the floor button behind her, then pulled her against his chest, letting the tree fall against the elevator wall as he kissed her. She leaned into him, opening her mouth to his searching tongue and welcoming him into the hot, wet corners of her mouth. He branded her lips with his, slanting them over hers again and again, their teeth clashing, their panted breath swapping and mingling, their sighs and moans making a chorus of desire.

When the bell rang and the doors opened, Eleanora stepped back from him, looking up at his eyes.

"What was that for?" he asked, his voice breathless and husky.

"Because you make me happy," she answered, taking the top of the tree in her hands and backing out of the elevator.

They placed the tree between two large windows in Tom's living room, and once it was decorated, he made a fire in the fireplace and turned off all the other lights in the apartment, so that the only light was the soft white from the tree and a flood of warm firelight.

Eleanora made scrambled eggs with cheese and sausage for dinner, and they ate it on a blanket under the lights—she called it a Christmas tree picnic—and Tom had insisted on opening a bottle of champagne and toasting the chef.

"Sorry about breakfast-for-dinner," she said, spooning eggs onto his empty plate.

"No complaints here," he said, digging in with gusto.

"I never learned to cook much. We made do with a lot of heated-up cans, you know? I really only learned to cook when I moved to Vail."

"Oh," he said, looking up at her with understanding. "You learned to cook at Auntie Rose's Breakfast-All-Day Chalet."

"Exactly." She pushed the eggs around on her plate, and he sensed she was feeling sheepish, but suddenly her expression brightened and she looked up at him. "But I can make almost any breakfast food you can think of. Pancakes. Waffles. Sausage, bacon, biscuits. Omelets. Eggs any way you want them . . ."

Her voice trailed off as he looked into her eyes. The reflection of the Christmas lights shone back at him. It was like she was lit up from the inside, and his heart throbbed when he answered, "I'll eat them any way you make them, Eleanora. I'll just be glad it's you giving them to me."

Her cheeks had reddened then, and they'd finished the rest of their dinner admiring the tree, then lying on their backs beneath it, side by side.

At some point, Tom had taken her hand in his, weaving their fingers together and resting them on his chest, over his heart.

"Eleanora?"

"Hmm?"

"Do you want me to tell you a little bit about tomorrow? About meeting with my grandfather?"

She squeezed his fingers. "Okay."

"Our family estate is called Haverford Park. My grandparents still live there. My father grew up there. So did I. When my parents divorced, my father took an apartment here in Philly, and after college, so did I. But Haverford Park will be mine one day."

"It's a mansion?"

"Yes. There are several acres of land, gardens, and a pool. We have six horses that are housed in the stables, and there's a stocked pond for trout fishing. There's a lawn for cricket and a gatehouse where the gardener lives with his wife. Our chauffeur and house staff live in apartments over the garage."

"Oh," she sighed, sounding out of breath. She tried to pull her hand away, but Tom held it tighter.

"You come from no Christmas tree and cans heated up for dinner. I come from . . . Haverford Park. Two different worlds, but as far as I'm concerned, neither one is better or worse than the other. We can't help where we come from, okay?"

She was silent for a long moment, but he felt her hand gradually relax until it readjusted to clasp his again. "Okay."

He took a deep breath, grateful that she didn't jump up and run away at the prospect of what she was walking into tomorrow.

"My grandfather is expecting us at three. I have to be honest: he wasn't pleased about meeting you. I should warn you, he could be rude about it . . . about us."

"About *me*," she corrected him.

"About the situation. A whirlwind marriage."

She threaded and rethreaded her fingers through his. "I can handle it."

He heard the tremor in her voice and rushed to reassure her. "I'll be right beside you. I won't . . . I mean, I won't let it get out of control."

"Don't worry," she said, rolling to her side to face him. "But let's not talk about it anymore, okay? Tomorrow will be here soon enough."

He rolled to mirror her, their hands still clasped together between them. Reaching out, he traced the lines of her face with the tips of his fingers.

"Thank you for doing this," he said.

"Don't thank me yet," she joked, but her eyes, heavy with apprehension, betrayed her.

He lowered his voice, his tone serious as he stared into her eyes. "You promised me, remember? No matter what happens with my grandfather, we'll talk about what happens with *us* after we leave Haverford tomorrow," he said, stroking her cheek, marveling at her heart-wrenching beauty. "Promise me again, Eleanora."

"I promise," she whispered, closing her eyes and leaning forward to tuck her head under his chin. She sighed deeply, and her voice was drowsy when she added, a few minutes later, "Merry Christmas, Tom. Thank you for the tree."

"You're welcome, sunshine," he murmured, pressing his lips to his wife's forehead.

He pulled their picnic blanket around them, then put his arm over her hips, drawing her up against his body. They didn't talk anymore. For now, there was nothing more to say. He held her until she fell asleep under their first Christmas tree, and after praying to God that tomorrow wouldn't be the end for them, Tom surrendered to sleep too.

Chapter 8

Eleanora squeezed Tom's hand as he helped her out of his sleek sports car, trying not to hyperventilate as she looked up at the dozens of windows of Haverford Park, which was roughly the size of the grandest hotel in Vail.

She smoothed her plain, black, ankle-length skirt and straightened the shoulder pads on her lavender silklike blouse. Suddenly her best clothes felt cheap, and she wished that she had something truly classy to wear, like real pearls or an elegant winter coat. She pulled the lapels of her bargain-bin coat closer and squeezed Tom's hand again.

"Don't be nervous," he said, leaning down close to her ear. "His bark is worse than his bite."

Tom reached forward to ring the bell, and a pretty young woman in a maid's outfit answered the door. "Tom!"

"Susannah! Merry Christmas!"

"To you too! And happy birthday!"

Eleanora smiled at the woman, who looked curiously at her.

"Susannah Edwards, this is Eleanora . . . my wife."

Susannah's eyes jerked back to Tom's in shock, but a delighted smile soon followed, and she extended her hand to Eleanora. "Oh, I'm so happy for you! Congratulations!"

"Thank you, Susannah," said Eleanora, feeling just a little bit better and more confident after such a warm greeting. "You're very kind."

"I'm happy for Tom," said Susannah, patting him on the arm before beaming at Eleanora. "And for you."

"Is my grandfather waiting for us?"

"He is," said Susannah, her grin fading as she turned to Tom. Her voice was cool and formal when she added, "Follow me, please."

Eleanora gulped as they walked down an austere hallway decorated with painted portraits and brass sconces. The entire house was like a museum—old and grand. And this is where Tom had grown up.

You come from no Christmas tree and cans heated up for dinner. I come from . . . Haverford Park. Two different worlds, but as far as I'm concerned, neither one is better or worse than the other. We can't help where we come from, okay?

She was determined not to judge him, just as he hadn't judged her. Yes, they were from two different worlds, but the only thing that mattered was how they felt about each other.

"It'll be okay," Tom whispered.

She nodded at him with her bravest smile. "I know it will."

Susannah knocked on a large, dark-wood door, and a gruff voice commanded, "Come!" She pushed open the door and gave Eleanora an encouraging smile, mouthing, "Good luck."

Pulled by Tom into his grandfather's study, Eleanora took a moment to glance around the room. The walls were covered with bookcases from floor to ceiling, and several easy chairs and love seats were placed around the enormous room for reading. In the center, in front of one massive window that looked out over the grounds of Haverford Park, was a large wooden desk. Behind it sat an older man—maybe in his seventies—with white hair and bushy eyebrows, wearing a three-piece suit and a maroon bow tie. He eyed Eleanora shrewdly, and she forced herself not to look away.

"Grandfather," said Tom, approaching the desk. "Merry Christmas."

"Yes, yes."

"You look well."

"Humph. I feel old." He gestured to the two stiff-backed chairs in front of the desk. "Sit."

Tom pulled out the left chair, and Eleanora sat down, folding her hands in her lap and staring at the elder Mr. English. If she looked down, it might convey that she was frightened or that she wasn't committed to Tom, and she didn't want that. She'd promised to help him secure his inheritance, and that's precisely what she intended to do.

"Who's this?" the older man asked gruffly, flicking a glance at Tom before looking back at Eleanora.

"Grandfather, may I present Eleanora Watters English, my bride?"

Mr. English stared at her with narrowed eyes for several long minutes. "She's a looker."

"Yes, sir," said Tom, a hint of pride in his voice.

"Where are you from, Miss Watters?"

"Colorado, sir."

"Whereabouts?"

"Romero."

"Never heard of it."

"That's not surprising. It's very small."

"Does everyone in Romero marry strangers on a whim?"

Eleanora swallowed.

Tom reached for her hand, and his grandfather huffed in disgust. "Save that for when you're alone."

She was relieved when Tom threaded his fingers through hers in defiance, anchoring her to him.

"What do you do for work, gal?"

"I'm a . . ." Her cheeks flushed with shame as she glimpsed a collection of silver trophies on a credenza behind the desk, but she lifted her chin. "I'm a waitress."

"Of course you are," said Mr. English, taking a deep breath and sighing. He shuffled some papers around on his desk without looking up. "Will you excuse us, Miss Watters?"

He was dismissing her? Just like that? Her heart thundered in her chest, a mix of indignance and nerves.

"Sir?"

"I'd like a word alone with my grandson now."

Cheeks burning, she disengaged her hand from Tom's and stood up. Her pocketbook, which had been resting on her lap, slid to the floor with a plop. She bent over to pick it up, fumbling with trembling fingers to pull it over her shoulder. Suddenly, she felt Tom's comforting hand on her arm, helping her up and walking her to the door.

"You did great," he whispered, though his eyes were flinty and flat. "Wait for me outside, okay?"

She nodded at him, trying not to cry.

She *hadn't* done great.

That much was clear.

"She's a looker, but is she also a hooker?"

Tom turned from the door to face his grandfather with barely restrained fury. The old man had done everything short of blatantly insulting Eleanora to her face, and Tom had never felt so angry with anyone in his life. "What the hell is the matter with you?"

"Is she?"

"No! She's a waitress!"

"Humph. Regardless, she's not at all what I had in mind for you."

"Be that as it may, she's my *wife*."

"Ha! Your *wife!* What a joke. She's cheap goods, is what *she* is. You met the girl five minutes ago, Thomas."

"That's enough!" Tom slapped his palms on his grandfather's desk, leaning over the dark mahogany to sneer at him. "Not only did I play by your rules, old man, but she's a better *woman* than any I've ever known. I'm lucky to be with her, and if anyone is cheap goods here, it's you, out of line with your cheap, below-the-belt shots."

"A Vegas wedding to a common waitress with no family, no education, no breeding." Tom's grandfather narrowed his eyes, sitting back in his desk chair and tenting his fingers under his chin. "You think you outsmarted me, boy? You didn't. You know as well as I do that you're thumbing your nose at my rules. But you're young, and you've always been a little impulsive, so I'll give you a chance to make things right. Annul this sham of a marriage and I will give you six more months to find someone appropriate before I cut you off."

Tom lifted his hands from the desk, crossing his arms over his chest. His grandfather gestured toward his office door with his chin.

"But I will require that *she* return to Colorado and *you* remain in Philadelphia, Thomas. So don't think you can annul the marriage and still have your cheap piece of ass on the side." He raised his bushy eyebrows. "So? What do you say? More than fair, eh?"

"What do I say?" Tom took a deep breath and tried to steady his voice, but it was still lethal. "I say, I'll take my chances with her. I say, keep your goddamn money. I don't want it. I say, I choose her." He turned around and strode across the office toward the door.

"Now, Thomas," the old man blustered, leaning forward to stand up.

"Forgive me, Grandfather," said Tom, turning the door-knob before he faced his aging relative one last time, "but go to hell."

Slamming the office door shut behind him, Tom looked right and left down the hallway, but Eleanora was nowhere to be seen.

"Eleanora?" he called.

"Psssht! Tom!" Susannah peeked out of the front parlor with a feather duster in her hand, beckoning him to come closer. "She left."

"She lef—wait. Why?"

Susannah winced. "I'm afraid your grandfather's office door wasn't closed very tightly. The whole house heard what he had to say about her."

Tom grimaced, clenching his eyes shut for a moment and taking a deep breath in an attempt to calm his fury. "Where'd she go?"

"She raced out the front door." Susannah offered Tom a sympathetic smile. "Bet you can still catch her."

"Thanks, Susannah," said Tom, racing for the door and swinging it open. He paused on the front steps of the mansion for a moment and spotted her—a speck in the distance at the end of the long, gravel driveway, almost at the gatehouse.

"Eleanora!"

Tom took off at a sprint, but she didn't slow down. She reached the gates and struggled to pull the heavy wrought iron open, finally managing to slip through. He ran as fast as he could, pulling open one of the gates and racing onto Blueberry Lane, where he found her leaning against a brick pillar at the entrance of the estate, her shoulders hunched forward and head down.

He stepped in front of her, reaching for her. "Eleanora."

She didn't look at him. Tears fell from her cheeks, plopping on the ground at their feet. "Please let me go."

"I can't," he said breathlessly.

"Please, Tom," she sobbed. "I have a credit card that I use for emergencies, and if I can j-just get to the airport, I can—"

Pulling her roughly against him, he crushed her to his chest, wrapping his arms around her and pressing his lips to her sweet-smelling hair. "Please don't go. You can't go. I told him to shove his money up his ass. I told him to go to hell. I told him I choose you, sunshine. I choose us."

She whimpered against his neck, a small, keening sound that broke his heart even as her body relaxed against his. "Tom . . ."

"I don't . . ." He inhaled raggedly, still trying to catch his breath. "I don't have all the answers, Eleanora. Maybe six months from now, you'll think I'm a prick and leave. Maybe I'll find out you're crazy and beg you to go. But right here? Right now? I want you. I want you so bad, I can't think straight. I want you so much, I just turned down fifteen million dollars. Like it or lump it, you're my wife, and I just . . . God, I just want to give us a chance."

"You do?" she asked softly, her voice still a little shaky.

"I do."

She leaned back, looking up at him with glistening eyes and a brilliant smile. "I want you too, Tom. So much."

He placed his palms on her cheeks and found her lips with his, parting them, claiming them, celebrating that they wouldn't have to say good-bye, that for now they had chosen each other, and feeling breathlessly excited for their future.

When they were both panting and trembling, he rested his forehead against hers. "You're worth it."

"God, I hope so," she murmured, laughing softly, her breath landing on his lips like a blessing.

"We'll have to move," he said. "That penthouse belongs to my family."

"I've been comfortable with a lot less."

"I have several thousand dollars of my own money saved up. I'm not broke," he said. "And I have a good education. I can apply for jobs in New York or Hartford maybe. I've worked at English & Son for years—I should be able to find something on Wall Street or in insurance. We'll find a little place. Start small, but fresh."

"I'll make it homey with very little. I know how to do that. And I'll have breakfast-for-dinner waiting for you every night when you come home."

"Every night that you don't have classes, you mean. You're finishing college, Eleanora. Between my savings and whatever I bring home, we'll make it happen. You could go to NYU or Columbia. We'll check them out this spring and enroll you for the fall term. Deal?"

She laughed softly again, leaning forward to kiss him. "Deal."

"I swear to you, I won't stop working until we're on our feet. I'll give you a good life. I promise if you take a chance on me, you won't regret it."

"But what about you?"

"What do you mean?"

She leaned back a little to gaze up at him, her smile fading, her fingers clasping his wrist.

"What about the money? How can you do this? How can you turn it down for me?"

"I want you more."

"Won't you resent me?"

"No, sunshine," he said softly, threading his fingers through her hair and kissing her tenderly. "And besides, maybe he'll come around one day. Once he knows you. Once he sees that he was right all along."

"*Right*?" she demanded, jerking back from him, her eyes wide and insulted. "What exactly was he *right* about?"

He ran the backs of his fingers across her cheek, soothing her. "'A good woman makes a man honest, makes him work harder, makes him true.' His words. That's why he wanted me to get married. His goal all along was for me to find a woman who made me honest and true, who made me want to work hard for her comfort, for her happiness." He pressed a sweet, swift kiss to her warmed-honey lips. "And he was right. A good woman can change the entire course of your life . . . if you want her badly enough . . . if you let her."

She was staring up at him, her eyes searching and fraught, determining if his words were true. Her tongue darted out to wet her lips, and she sucked her bottom lip between her teeth for a moment before letting it go. And that was the moment—he watched it happen before his very eyes— that was the moment Eleanora Watters *became* Eleanora English.

"I'm going to fall in love with you," she whispered. "I'm going to give you the big family you want. I'm going to be sure you never, ever regret choosing me. I promise, Tom. That's my promise to you: I'll spend the rest of my life making you happy too."

"A dream and a miracle," he murmured, drawing her back against him and closing the distance between their lips.

An Interlude

Haverford Park
Christmastime 2015

". . . and he whispered, 'A dream and a miracle.'" Eleanora English sighed as her daughter-in-law, Emily Edwards English, handed her another ornament, which she fastened onto a sturdy pine branch. "The end."

The room was so silent, you could have heard a pin drop, and then . . .

"Wait! *What*?" exclaimed Jessica Winslow English, the wife of Eleanora's third son, Alex. "What do you mean 'the *end*'?"

Eleanora turned around to find six younger women—her husband's niece, Kate, plus her sons' wives and significant others—staring at her with their mouths gaping open in various states of disbelief and indignation. She had invited the girls over for a tree-trimming party at Haverford Park this year, and was enjoying every moment with these smart, funny, wonderful women. When Molly, the brand-new fiancée of her fifth son, Weston, had asked to hear the story of how her future in-laws had met, Eleanora couldn't help indulging them and had been spinning the tale for over an hour.

"The end," said Eleanora again, gesturing uselessly with one hand. "Um . . . *the end* of the story."

"I don't think so," said Valeria with a little bit of attitude. She was the girlfriend of Eleanora's fourth son, Stratton, and the most outspoken of the girls. Eleanora absolutely adored her for it because she'd pulled shy Stratton out of his shell and loved him for exactly who he was. "You can't just end it like that."

"What do you mean?"

Molly cocked her head to the side. "You're really leaving us hanging, Eleanora. Did they move to New York? Did he find a job? Were they happy? What about Evie and Van?"

"Good question," said Daisy Edwards English, her second son Fitz's wife, who had just been upstairs to check on her daughter—Eleanora's first grandchild—baby Caroline. Daisy picked up a plate of homemade cookies from the coffee table and handed them to her cousin, Emily. "We have to know what happened to ditzy, darling Evie! Did they end up together?"

Jessica pursed her lips, turning to Eleanora's niece by marriage. "Kate, did you *know* your great-grandfather?"

"He sounds like a real piece of work," added Valeria.

"Thankfully, no," said Kate English-almost-Rousseau, looking disgusted. "He died before I was born. But my dad is much younger than Uncle Tom, and they had different mothers."

"Did Tom ever get the money?" asked Jessica, turning back to Eleanora.

Eleanora grinned at her, and Jessica turned her sharp, green eyes to Emily. "Susannah's *your* mother, Emily. Did you ever meet Evie? Do you know how the story ends?"

Emily shrugged, shaking her head. "I can't ever remember meeting someone named Evie. And even though I've lived at Haverford Park for most of my life, I promise I've never even *heard* this story. Please, Eleanora, you've got to tell us the rest!"

Valeria leaned an elbow on Jessica's shoulder. "No more ornaments until we get the rest of the story, Eleanora."

Molly tucked an errant strand of red hair behind her ear, looking hopeful. Her enormous engagement ring caught the firelight and glistened merrily. "There's a fresh thermos of hot cocoa here. We could take a break from decorating, and you could tell us the rest?"

Emily and Daisy had already cuddled up together on the overstuffed couch, and Molly squeezed in beside Daisy. Kate poured them all steaming mugs of cocoa, and Valeria sat cross-legged on the floor in front of the fire. Jessica, still standing beside the tree with her hands on her hips, shrugged at her mother-in-law with a saucy grin as she gestured to the armchair by the fire.

"Fine! You girls win," said Eleanora, laughing as she sat down and accepted a steaming cup of chocolate from Kate. "But I warn you, 'the course of true love—'"

"'—never did run smooth,'" finished Valeria gently. "That's okay. We still want to know."

Jessica sat down on the love seat next to Kate, and Eleanora took a deep breath, thinking back, remembering what came next. Her eyes teared for just a moment, but she took another deep breath.

"We were falling in love. We were . . . full of hope," she started, letting her memories carry her away.

Chapter 9

Haverford Park
Christmas Eve, 1981

Eleanora and Tom walked back up the driveway toward Tom's car, their hands bound together as gleaming, white gravel crunched under their feet. Eleanora's mind was spinning from the decision they'd just made together: Tom had turned down fifteen million dollars—an almost unfathomable sum of money—so that he could give their two-day marriage a chance.

It felt foolish and reckless, and his impetuousness frightened her.

It also made her heart swell with tenderness and her body tremble with longing.

Eleanora had never been anyone's first choice for anything. How in the world did she find herself here—with a man who had, literally, chosen *her* over diamonds and gold?

Looking up at the austere exterior of Haverford Park, she gulped, counting the sparkling windows nervously as she wondered if Grandfather English was watching them and hoping he wasn't. He was a hateful, hurtful old man who'd judged her before knowing her, and she couldn't wait to get back into Tom's car and leave Haverford for good.

She'd just asked him, *What about the money? How can you do this? How can you turn it down for me?* And he'd sweetly—and resolutely—answered, *I want you more.*

Clutching his hand more tightly as they approached the car, she made him stop and face her, ignoring the tears that blurred her vision.

"Are you *sure*, Tom?"

He glanced up at the old house, narrowing his eyes and tightening his jaw before looking down at her upturned face with such gentleness, she couldn't keep the tears from spilling over the edges of her eyes.

He nodded, using his thumbs to swipe at the wetness before it could wind down her face.

"Positive."

A quiet surge of pure joy lifted her heels from the ground as she wrapped her arms around his neck and pulled him down to kiss her. His arms—so strong and so certain, it twisted her heart—pulled her against his solid body, her thrift-shop coat colliding with his caramel-colored cashmere.

The kiss lasted only a moment before Tom rested his cold cheek against hers, still clutching her tightly.

"We'll be okay, sunshine. I promise."

"You don't know what it's like," she said softly, looking over his shoulder at a tennis court and a swimming pool in the distance, "to be poor."

"We won't be poor," he said. "I have some savings, and as soon as I get a job, we'll have a decent income too."

"You don't know what it's like to be alone," she pressed on, fearful for him, "without family."

"Believe me, a crotchety grandfather, an ineffective father, and a kid brother I barely know don't constitute a family. Somehow I think I'll get by." He leaned back, grinning at her. "Plus, I have you, baby. You're my family now."

She clenched her eyes shut against the welcome sweetness of his words, rubbing her cheek against his soft shoulder as tears ran over the bridge of her nose and plopped onto his expensive coat.

"Let's go," he rumbled near her ear. "I want to be alone with my family."

She heard the humor in his voice, but also the hunger, and she sucked in a deep breath as she realized how desperately she wanted to be alone with him too—in his bed, underneath his body, sharing the most private parts of herself with him.

"Me too," she said, pulling away from him and wiping her eyes.

"Smile for me," he said, cupping her cheeks in his cold hands. "It's my birthday."

Tomorrow she would think about their future.

Tomorrow she would close the floodgates to the overwhelming waves of emotion that so compromised her common sense today.

Tomorrow she would rationally explore what lay before them and try to figure out how best to conserve what resources they had until Tom found a job and they landed on their feet.

But today? Today she was Mrs. Thomas English—someone's wife, someone wanted, someone precious . . . someone who, judging by the dark look in her husband's eyes and the growly way he said he wanted to be alone with her, wasn't going to get a wink of sleep tonight.

She couldn't have stopped herself if she tried.

She beamed at Tom as he helped her into his car.

It's not that Tom *only* wanted to jump his wife . . .

        . . . but that Tom *absolutely* wanted to jump his wife.

From the moment he'd seen her, giving a wiseass tourist what for in the restaurant where she used to waitress, he'd wanted her. Eleanora Watters English was young and stunning—her body slim but curvy, her hair a natural blonde, her eyes a bright blue, and her lips a pink and pillowed marvel. He'd kissed her more times than he could count now, but his body was starving for more.

He wanted to kiss more than her lips. He wanted to touch his tongue to every secret valley of her body until she writhed beneath him, begging him to slide into her waiting heat and take her to paradise. He wanted those gorgeous lips clamped around his swollen sex, her eyes soft and dark as she sucked him to the point of madness and allowed him to finish down her throat. He wanted her tits in his mouth, her nipples pebbled and proud as he licked them into hard points. He wanted to hear the noises she made as she came— and feel the way her body tightened around his, squeezing him, milking him, taking everything he wanted to give her, until they were both sated and exhausted, wrapped bonelessly around one another until dawn.

But he also wanted her to understand how precious she was to him. How his fists had clenched with the certainty of his renunciation of his grandfather. How his breathing had almost stopped when he realized she'd fled, and how his heart had swelled with protectiveness and gratitude when he saw her small body at the gates of Haverford Park. She had asked him—three times now—if he was sure about his decision to turn his back on his fortune, and she couldn't possibly understand the sense of freedom and satisfaction he was presently enjoying. She had given him a reason to finally say no, to break the oppressive English yoke around his neck and choose a different course for his life. She was his angel, his reason, his salvation, and his partner.

Yes, he wanted to *fuck* her.

But more importantly, for the first time in his life, his mind, heart, and body were one in the all-consuming need to *make love* to a woman.

To his *wife*, who, he realized, was riding along beside him in utter silence.

"Eleanora?"

"Hmm?" she murmured, turning her head to look at him.

And again, as always, his world was rocked by her beauty—the flawless perfection of her skin, the dusting of freckles over her nose, the alertness in her blue eyes.

I will never tire of this face, he vowed wordlessly. *I will always strive to see happiness and pride in these eyes.*

And love? whispered his heart.

He cleared his throat.

He wasn't ready to apply the word *love* to their situation yet.

"Yes?" she prompted.

"Umm . . ." His mind had scattered, *love* reverberating like an iron pipe hitting another iron pipe behind his eyes. "Stores'll be closing soon. Need anything?"

She glanced at the dashboard, where the clock read "3:45," and nodded. "Can you stop at a grocery store? I'll get a few things for tomorrow."

He nodded, marveling at the simple domesticity of her request.

"I've never . . ." he started, then winced.

"Never what?" she asked.

"Never been inside a grocery store," he admitted.

"What?" Her jaw dropped, and she gaped at him. "How is that *possible*?"

Grinning at her, he shrugged. "Always had someone else to go, I guess. And most of them deliver."

"For a fee!" she cried, laughing softly as she shook her head.

To his shame, he had no idea what grocery stores charged to deliver food. It had never really crossed his mind to find out either.

"Well," she said crisply, smoothing her black skirt, "at some point soon, I will give you your first tour of a grocery store. But tonight, I go alone."

"You'd deprive me of watching you shop?"

"I don't *shop*," she said, her eyes serious. "I choose carefully—only things I need—and then I pay for them before I can be tempted to buy anything else."

"You don't have to do that anymore," he said.

She sighed. "You don't have a new job yet."

"But I will."

"I know," she said lightly, giving him a sweet smile. "But I have my own reasons for going solo tonight." He pulled into a parking spot at an A&P and kept the engine running. She leaned over the bolster and kissed him quickly. "I'll only be a minute."

The door slammed, and he watched her go—her black boots barely touching down on the wet pavement, her steps nimble and certain. And she was his. *His* wife.

The word left him breathless, and his chest swelled with pride. He looked to his right and left, hoping to see some other young husband waiting for his new wife, with whom he could share a knowing grin and wink that said *Yes, she's mine. Do you know this kind of happiness, brother?* But the cars on either side of him were empty. Everyone was inside, bustling about, buying Christmas groceries in an unknown store the size of a football field filled with food.

It was absurd that he'd never been inside a grocery store, and he mused, for just a moment, about the changes imminent in his life. For all of his adulthood, Tom had had access to a trust fund that had allowed him a truly luxurious lifestyle. A new car for New Year's? Sure! Skiing in Zermatt at a

week's notice? Absolutely! Purchases weren't considered—
they were made. Country club membership fees were paid;
the mortgage on his penthouse, which technically belonged
to the English Family Trust, had been paid in full over fifty
years ago, when his grandfather was a twenty-something
financial wunderkind.

As much as he didn't want to think about it, let alone
admit it, Eleanora was right. Things were going to change.

With his savings of several thousand dollars, they could
find an apartment in any city, pay the first and last months'
rent, and live comfortably, if not luxuriously, for two or three
months. But the money would eventually run out. Now, if
Tom used his family and college connections to secure a job
on Wall Street or in one of the Hartford insurance agencies
that he'd dealt with professionally for years, he could assume
a lifestyle of wealth and comfort that wouldn't include a new
car every January, but wouldn't prohibit one every two or
three years, either. It would be a different life for Tom—
more modest, less luxurious, but still steeped in comfort.
And anyway, Eleanora might not like a stupendously rich
lifestyle—surely modest wealth and comfort would be more
palatable to her.

Besides, it was a temporary lifestyle, wasn't it? He narrowed his eyes as the snow began to fall, adding a chill to
the warmth of his musings. One day, when his grandfather
arrived on their doorstep and begged Eleanora's forgiveness
on his knees, their fortune would be restored.

"And write 'Happy Birthday, Tom' on it, okay?" she asked the
baker. "Do you have candles?"

He nodded at her, his smile lazy and appreciative. "Of
course, pretty lady. Aisle 12. With the greeting cards."

She nodded at him, ignoring his borderline-lecherous looks. A card was a great idea. "I'll be back in a few minutes for the cake, okay?"

Without waiting for his response, she turned around, checking out the contents of her wire basket as she walked briskly to the cards: orange juice, a dozen eggs, shredded cheddar, sausage, Wonder Bread, milk, pancake mix, Crisco, bananas, butter, and maple syrup. She planned to make a casserole tonight, soaking the white bread in whisked eggs and crumbled sausage, then topping it with cheese. Tomorrow, when she baked it, it would be as light and fluffy as a soufflé. And tonight, for his birthday, she'd make banana pancakes with butter and syrup—so thin, they could almost be crepes. They were her two best dishes, and for Tom's birthday and their first Christmas together, she wanted everything to be as perfect as possible.

Turning down the stationery aisle, she looked for the birthday cards, finally stopping before the ones marked "Husband" with widened eyes. She set her basket on the floor and rubbed her hands together, willing them to reach out and take a card. Her fingers trembled as they touched lightly over the cards on the top row, but she couldn't seem to choose one.

My Darling Beloved Spouse . . .

To the Father of My Children: I'd Choose You All Over Again . . .

To the Man Who's Been With Me Through Thick and Thin . . .

For My Soul Mate: I'd Be Lost Without You . . .

They all felt too heavy-handed for Tom, and suddenly she felt like a child who pretends to be a princess by wearing dress-up, for whom the illusion is shattered when her mother calls to her to set the table or take out the garbage. Here she was, in bona fide Wife Land, and she felt nothing like a wife. It's not that she felt like an impostor either, and maybe she'd feel differently after they'd consummated their marriage—but mostly she just felt new. And young. And, to her great shame, as she considered Tom's sacrifice, uncertain.

Finally, she dropped her hands, her fingers playing nervously with the simple, gold band on her ring finger as she took a step back in defeat.

And then she saw it:

Two hands clasped together, with the sunset behind them, and the words *The most perfect place in the world* . . . Eleanora reached for the card and opened it, whispering aloud, ". . . is anywhere with you. Happy Birthday, with love."

She hadn't realized that she was holding her breath until she released it, then drew in another, and it was stilted and ragged with emotion because the words felt so right. Tom wasn't the only person who'd given up his life, she thought, plucking an envelope from behind the small stack of cards and adding both to her basket, careful not to get them wet. Eleanora had given up her life too—living with and looking after her cousin in Vail, college, and independence. Not that she believed Tom would begrudge her visits with her meager family, and he'd already insisted that her education would be one of their priorities as couple, but surely she was giving up her independence, wasn't she? Yes. She was. Whatever dreams she'd had as a single girl were gone for now, as she and Tom tried to make a go of marriage.

And yet, she thought, picking up the cake without looking at the baker and making her way to the checkout, she was exactly where she wanted to be. She'd chosen Tom, not the other way around. She'd asked to bind her destiny to his, to marry him. And when he finally did choose her this afternoon—to the exclusion of his family—she'd chosen him again.

Yes, I want you against the odds. You choose me? Well, guess what? I choose you too.

She handed the cashier her emergency credit card and signed her name to the receipt, taking her bags and walking out of the store. And there was Tom, pulled up close to the curb, no doubt because snow had started to fall.

His eyes met hers through the passenger window, and he grinned at her as she opened the door.

"You're back," he said.

"You doubted?"

"No," he said, pulling away from the store. "I'm just happy to see you."

She smiled back at him before turning to her window to watch the snow fall. And in a rare state of perfect contentment, she heard the words in her head and knew they were true:

The most perfect place in the world . . . is anywhere with you.

Tom had taken the two grocery bags from Eleanora as they walked into his building from the car, but she shooed him from the kitchen when he tried to help her unpack them. So banished, he headed back to his bedroom for a few minutes. A nervous energy, fueled by today's daring and in anticipation of his time alone with Eleanora, made Tom straighten up and make his bed—something he hadn't done in years, since his building employed a maid service. But the service didn't come on Christmas Eve, so Tom plumped the pillows and straightened the sheets on his own, then bent down to gather up his laundry and place it in the bathroom hamper. He brushed his teeth and briefly considered lighting the two candles he found in his medicine chest, but he heard

Eleanora call his name and wiped off his mouth quickly, heading back to the living room.

She stood in front of their Christmas tree in her black skirt and lavender blouse. She'd kicked off her boots, but her feet were dark in black panty hose. Holding two glasses of red wine, she held one out to him, and that's when he noticed the little cake, covered with a blaze of candles, on his coffee table.

"Happy birthday," she said, smiling at him as she lifted her glass to clink his.

"Is this what you bought in the grocery store?" he asked.

"Among other things." She nodded, bending down to place her glass on the table and lift the little cake. "Everyone should have a cake on his birthday."

He laughed softly, trying to remember the last time a woman had had his name written on a birthday cake, and his smile faded when he realized it was probably his fourth birthday, when his mother was still in the picture. Such frivolities hadn't been part of Haverford Park celebrations after she left. His birthday had been celebrated with a donation to a local charity in his name and a brief, perfunctory salutation at breakfast.

"Is it okay?" Eleanora asked.

He nodded, overcome with emotion, unable to trust his own voice.

"Then make a wish," she encouraged him.

"It already came true," he whispered, holding her eyes as he blew out the candles.

His declaration changed the electricity between them from playful to intense, and he set his glass down on the coffee table beside hers, then carefully took the cake from her hands, listening to the sound of her breathing as he placed it back on the serving plate.

When he straightened, her eyes were wide and dark, full of promise and invitation. Tom reached for her face, placing his palm gently on her cheek, his body tightening as she closed her eyes and leaned into his touch.

"I'm crazy about you," he said softly, his voice thick and gravelly with lust and tenderness and wanting it to be good for her, and him, and . . . and . . .

Her eyes opened slowly, and her tongue darted out to lick her lips. "Then kiss me."

Chapter 10

Flattening her hands on his chest, she felt the strength of him through his shirt and undershirt, the ripples of toned muscles, the certain, steady pressure of his lungs as he breathed her in, sucking her tongue into his mouth and groaning softly.

From the moment they'd walked back up the driveway of Haverford Park hand in hand, Eleanora had known this moment was coming. She'd been nervous, of course, but her feelings for Tom—and her pure, undiluted lust for him—overpowered any notions of backing away or putting on the brakes. She wasn't a wanton woman, but she wanted him every bit as badly as he wanted her.

Sliding her fingers to the lapels of his navy suit jacket, she pushed it over his broad shoulders, listening as it dropped to the floor. As he ravaged her mouth with his, her fingers skimmed to the buttons on his shirt. They trembled with nerves and longing as she opened each in its turn, one by one. Then, smoothing her hands down his arms, which tensed beneath her touch, she pushed the material to his wrists, where it got caught.

Leaning away from him, her lips slick and raw, she said, "Take it off."

"My shirt?"

"Everything," she whispered.

His face registered surprise at first, then he grinned at her as he unbuttoned his cuffs and let his shirt drop to the floor. Her fingers reached to pull his T-shirt from the waistband of his pants, but he covered her hands gently with his, stopping her.

"Eleanora?"

She gulped, her nerves taking over now that they'd stopped kissing and she'd more or less demanded that he strip. Taking a deep breath, she looked up into his intense, blue eyes.

"I have no problem getting naked for you, baby," he said, cupping her face with his hands. "And if you want fast, we'll go fast." His thumbs stroked her cheek, and she felt herself relaxing, melting, his touch stoking her desire. "Because whether it's now or later, I'll have you slow too. I'll have you so slow that every tremble, every gasp, every goose bump, will know where I've been and belong to me."

His thumb slipped into her mouth, and she sucked on it, trying to remember how to breathe. He rubbed the slick digit along her bottom lip, his eyes dark, almost fierce, as he stared down at her. Then he reached behind his neck and tugged his T-shirt over his head, baring his chest to her as she'd asked.

She dropped her eyes to his torso, noting that while it was muscular—he did, after all, ski—it wasn't oversculpted. Strong and dusted with blond hair, he was so beautiful in her eyes, she almost winced. Reaching out to touch him, the pads of her fingers alighted on his chest, and she flattened them, her palms covering his nipples, which beaded under her touch, making him groan softly.

Her eyes darted up, and his lips tilted up in a tender smile, even as his brows furrowed in an expression caught somewhere between pleasure and pain.

"Your turn," he said, holding her eyes as he slowly unbuttoned her blouse and spread it open. He ran his palms reverently along her collarbone, and the silk sluiced down her arms with a soft whoosh. Without asking, he pulled her into his arms, unfastening her bra and sliding the straps down to her wrists, then watching as they slipped to the floor.

Fighting the overwhelming urge to cover herself, Eleanora blinked her gaze away from him and closed her eyes as Tom's hands landed on her bare waist. As he raised them upward, he leaned forward, and his lips brushed against hers as the blond hair on his chest grazed her nipples. They tightened as though on command, puckering for him, straining shamelessly closer to the source of their pleasure. His hands bracketed her breasts as he deepened their kiss, running his tongue along the seam of her lips, which she opened willingly, welcoming his tongue to meet and mate with hers as his hands shifted, gently covering her naked breasts.

She moaned into his mouth, arching her back to thrust her breasts more fully against his hands, and he massaged them tenderly, circling his thumb around her erect nipple.

"Tom," she murmured as the sharp sensations started stealing her breath away.

Tom seized the moment as a chance to slide his lips down her throat to her chest, then lower, capturing one pert bud between his lips as his fingers teased its twin into a tight point. His other hand slid to the zipper at the back of her skirt and tugged it down so that her skirt slipped over her slim hips and pooled at her ankles, the cool air of his apartment touching her legs at the same time his teeth grazed her nipple.

She whimpered, reaching for his head and pulling it up to kiss her again, her hands skating between them as she searched for his belt buckle. Tom tilted his head, sealing his lips completely over hers, kissing her hungrily as she unfastened his belt, unbuttoned and quickly unzipped his pants.

He reached down and pushed them over his hips, then stepped out of them, reaching for Eleanora. Cupping her ass, he lifted her into his arms, and she kissed him madly as she wrapped her arms around his neck and her legs around his waist, her panties and stockings a frustrating barrier between his skin and hers.

Walking purposefully through his apartment as though she weighed nothing, Tom carried her away from their first Christmas tree, through the living room, down the back hallway, passing the guest bedroom and striding into his own. He didn't stop until he'd laid her down on the bed and covered her body with his, planting his elbows on either side of her head as he finished kissing her.

Finally, he drew back, cradling her face in his palms and looking down at her. The light was dim, but he could easily make out her features from the light streaming in through the hallway and from the windows, which had a direct view of Independence Mall.

Her eyes searched his.

"What?" she asked.

"Do you still want to go fast?"

Her lips tilted up into a grin. "This feels nice, whatever speed it is."

His cock, which throbbed behind his boxers, didn't agree. It wanted fast. It wanted now. But it was Tom's heart—the very heart that insisted upon making love in lieu of fucking—that kept him from taking her right this minute. He wanted these moments with her to last. He wanted their first time together to be memorable, to be . . . good.

"I care . . ." he started, then flinched at the word *care*. Wasn't there a better word? Something that came after like but before love? And if there was, what was it? How could he define the immensity of what he felt for her—his sweet, bright Eleanora, his sunshine, his wife. "I care about you very much."

Her smile widened just a touch because his stupid, half-assed, inaccurate declaration pleased her. "I know. I care about you, too."

"I didn't expect . . ." He cleared his throat, stroking her golden hair. "I didn't expect to fall for you so fast."

"Me neither."

"You're so young," he breathed, staring down at her loveliness. It made his chest tighten and his heart throb even worse than his cock. "I want to make you happy."

"Tom," she said, adjusting beneath him to cradle his erection in the soft valley between her thighs, "I've never been this happy in my life. Not in my whole life. When you blew out your candles tonight, you said your wish had already come true. Mine too. Being with you is a dream come true."

Her voice was thready and emotional as she finished her short speech, and Tom leaned down to nuzzle her nose gently, brushing his lips tenderly against hers and pushing his hips experimentally into hers.

She surged against him eagerly, meeting his shallow thrust and skimming her hands down the sides of her body to the waistband of her panty hose.

"Help me."

Tom shimmied backward, kneeling on either side of her thighs and gazing down at her as he slipped his fingers into the waistband of her panties.

"You sure?"

She arched an eyebrow in challenge. "Are you?"

His lips twitched under his mustache because he loved the way she could be nervous one moment, tender the next, and sassy as hell the moment after that.

He peeled the second skins away from her hips, which revealed a lightly swelled stomach that he ached to kiss . . . her pelvis and the tight thatch of light curls that made his balls fist . . . her thighs, which were toned and white in the moonlight . . . her gorgeous legs, ankles, and feet. And finally his wife was naked on his bed, beneath him, where he'd wanted her since the very first moment he laid eyes on her.

"You're breathtaking," he said.

"And a little chilly," she added, grinning at him.

He pulled his boxers quickly down his legs and threw them on the floor, then lowered his body to hers, skin to skin, his hard angles against her softness, his eager sex probing the damp, hidden depths of hers. As his cock slid over her clit, she whimpered softly, arching her back and burying her head back against his pillow.

"Tom," she moaned. "I want more."

He panted lightly, heat pooling below his stomach, stretching and swelling his already-straining erection. "Are you . . . baby, are you on the, um, the pill?"

"I, um," she sighed, pulling her lower lip between her teeth. "No."

"No?"

"No, I . . . I can't afford a prescription every month. Especially since . . ."

"Since?"

"I mean, I'm not like my cousin, Tom. I wasn't dating anyone seriously in Colorado. I didn't need monthly birth control."

As much as it pleased Tom to know that Eleanora hadn't been with anyone in a while, he also wasn't eager to get her pregnant.

"I don't have anything here," he said, rubbing against her, his body demanding more even though common sense was telling him to put on the brakes.

"You could, um, pull out," she said, cringing and quickly reaching up to cover her face with her hands, which was so adorable, he started chuckling lightly.

"Are you covering your face?"

"It's embarrassing," she said, her voice muffled under her arm.

"Baby, I hate to break it to you, but we're both buck naked in my bed, about to have sex. You don't have anything to be embarrassed about." She didn't move her arms from over her eyes, so he leaned down and peppered her arms with kisses until she did. Even in the moonlight, he could tell her cheeks were flushed and rosy.

"Not to mention," he said, grinning at her, though his voice was suddenly husky, "we're married. You're my wife. You don't have to be embarrassed about anything with me." He paused. "I can pull out."

"You don't mind?"

Hell, yes! I wanted to feel every inch of you.

"You're going on the pill tomorrow," he answered gruffly, reaching down between them to guide his cock into the valley of her clit. He glided against her, and she moaned.

"T-tomorrow's Christmas."

"The day after, then. As soon as possible."

"You're . . . bossy," she sighed, her body moving in rhythm with his, meeting his shallow thrusts, her breathing quick and ragged.

"You're delectable."

"I'm ready," she said, opening her eyes slowly. There was only a thin band of blue around her enormous, black irises. She licked her lips and widened her legs. "I want you, Tom."

It was all the permission he needed to pull back, readjust, then thrust forward slowly. The opening of her sex was hot and slick, and he held his breath, savoring the feel of her sucking him forward.

"Is this okay?" he asked in a strangled voice.

Her hands landed on his ass, and suddenly she surged up, her back arching, her fingers pushing him forward. "More."

He groaned, sliding forward into her completely, the walls of her sex pulsing and trembling around his erection, which swelled impossibly within her, throbbing with the immensity of his desire, with the sheer pleasure of being joined with her. The downside, however, to this much lust: one more thrust and he'd come.

"Next time," he ground out, pulling back, "I'll go slow."

He reached between their bodies, finding her pebbled nub of flesh just over the spot where they were so intimately connected, and he circled it, rubbing gently as he pushed back inside her body. His eyes clenched shut, any remaining self-control utterly gone as he felt the walls of her sex tighten around him, hold him, massage him while she cried out his name. He groaned with pleasure so sharp, so consuming, he didn't know how much more he could stand. *One more time. One more time.* Slowly, slowly, he slid back in, feeling the gathering, the tightening, the inevitable.

Jerking back just in time, he came in hot spurts on her stomach before pulling her into his arms so she could ride out her own orgasm clasped tightly against him.

When her body had finally stopped trembling, she sighed happily against his neck, her breath making his cock harden again like she'd placed an order.

"Shower?" she murmured softly, flattening her hands against his chest and pressing her lips to his throat.

"In a little bit," he answered, kissing her head. "Let me hold you for another minute or two."

"Mmmm," she sighed, snuggling against him.

And Tom, who'd known his wife for less than a week, realized that love—a word he'd been reluctant to use before now—didn't ask for permission. Sometimes it just arrived. Fully formed. And all you could do was hold on to it for dear life.

He tightened his arms around her and closed his eyes.

Eleanora's eyes blinked against the bright light of morning streaming in through Tom's bedroom windows. She rolled onto her side to face him, surprised to find his side of the bed empty, though still warm.

"Tom?" she called, sitting up gingerly, the tenderness between her legs making her grin like a hussy.

Pulling the sheet around her shoulders, she swung her legs over the side of the bed and padded out of his room, her bare feet soft on his hardwood floors. She could hear him speaking to someone from his office, across the hall from the guest room, and she followed his voice, stopping just outside the door.

"No, sir," he growled. "That request is unacceptable."

She furrowed her brows at his cold, angry tone.

"Because I've already made my decision, and I'm staying married."

Ah, she thought with a wince. *His grandfather, trying to make him reconsider.*

"I don't owe you an explanation. I'm a grown man."

There was a long pause, and Eleanora was just about to make her presence known by clearing her throat when she heard him exclaim, "He can't do that!"

She froze in place.

"Blackball his own *grandson*?" The disgust in his voice made her shiver, and she pulled the sheet more securely around herself, huddled unnoticed in the doorway. "In Boston and New York too? Well. He's really outdone himself."

Eleanora wasn't totally certain what *blackball* meant, but she felt it had to do with business matters, and she could tell from Tom's voice that it wasn't good. And he wasn't speaking to his grandfather, obviously, so she had to assume he was talking to his father. She couldn't bear hearing him struggle alone anymore, so she stepped inside his office, fixing a bright grin on her face when he looked up at her.

"Morning," she said softly, trembling inside as his bedsheets trailed behind her like a train.

His eyes, which were cold and annoyed when they looked up, softened immediately, his pursed lips loosened, tilting up in the smallest smile. She gestured to his lap, and he spun around in his desk chair so she could climb into his arms and rest her cheek against his chest. His heart thundered under her ear as he wrapped his arms around her.

Covering the mouthpiece of the telephone, he whispered, "I'll be done in a second."

"Take your time," she sighed.

"I fully comprehend the state of affairs, sir," he said, his voice cold again, but much sadder now. "Be that as it may, my decision still stands."

Eleanora pressed her lips to his neck, lingering there for a moment, breathing in the fresh, clean, showered, morning scent of her husband.

"I don't know, but I'll figure it out. Yes, we'll be out by tomorrow." He paused, his forehead falling onto her shoulder like a little boy who'd run too far from things too terrible to guess, and just wanted to rest in a safe and quiet place. "Thank you, sir. Merry Christmas to you, as well. Good-bye."

Taking a deep and ragged breath, Tom sighed heavily before reaching forward to place the phone back in the receiver, then he adjusted his arms around Eleanora, holding her tighter as he leaned back into his chair.

She let several seconds pass before kissing his neck again.

"Merry Christmas, husband," she said gently.

"Yeah," he said in a miserable voice. "Merry Christmas."

"You'll feel better if you tell me about it."

"I highly doubt that," he answered.

"Try me," she coaxed.

She felt him clench his jaw against the crown of her head, and the way his chest pushed against her body told her he was holding his breath. Finally, he exhaled.

"We need to move out of here by tomorrow."

"Fine. I'd prefer something smaller," she said, leaning back to look into his eyes. They were angry and sad and defeated, and she hated that so much, she could taste it. "Is that all?"

"No," he said, shaking his head, dropping her eyes, and furrowing his brows as if he'd received unbelievable or shocking news. "If I don't start the process to annul our marriage tomorrow, he's blackballing me."

"That doesn't sound good," she said, keeping her voice even.

"It's not. It means it'll be just about impossible for me to find a job with a bank or insurance agency on the East Coast. It means—"

"That we'll have to figure out something else."

"I'm a banker, Eleanora," he said softly. "That's who I am."

"Hmm," she said lightly. "I think you're more than that. You didn't study finance at Princeton. You studied English."

"Great. We'll both starve while I write poetry."

"*Did* you write poetry?" she asked, tilting her head to the side and grinning at him, despite this news that was clearly crushing him.

"Once upon a time," he said, dropping her eyes. "I'm sorry, baby. You married me for a million, and you're getting nothing."

Whip fast, she reached for his face, forcing him to meet her fierce, wide eyes. "Don't you *dare* say that! Don't you *ever* say that to me." Her voice trembled from the power of her feelings for him, of the hate she bore his grandfather, and of the contempt she felt for his father. "I got *you*, Tom. I got *you*, and that's all I want. We'll figure this out."

For a moment, his face turned hopeful, but his eyes flattened almost immediately. "We have to leave tomorrow, and I have no plan, Eleanora. None. My business contacts are useless. I don't . . . I just don't know what to do."

"I do," she said, lifting her chin and forcing a lighthearted grin, despite her worries for them. "I'm going to make breakfast. A good one that you're going to love and ask for every Christmas that we're together. And after that, we're going to climb back into your bed and make love all day. That'll be our present to each other."

"I have to say," he said, licking his lips before dropping his gaze to hers, "this is a really solid plan so far."

She grinned at him, momentum and hope gathering in her heart. "When we're both completely satisfied—"

"We have to be out *tomorrow*, not next week."

She chuckled. "We'll get all your suitcases together and start packing."

He nodded. "Right. Fine. Then what? We're fed, oversexed, and packed. Now for the hard part . . ."

"I assume we can keep your car?" she asked, letting the sheet fall a little until the tips of her pink areolas were revealed.

Tom's eyes dropped as fast as her skirt last night. "It's, uh . . . wow . . . yeah, it's paid off. It's mine."

Mine. And somehow she knew he wasn't talking about his car, and it made heat pool gloriously in her stomach. She let the sheet fall a little more until both of her breasts were exposed to the cool air of his office, her nipples puckering to dusky points as he reached up to cover one with his palm.

"Yours," she murmured.

"Then what?" he asked, plumping her breast before dropping his head and licking a slow circle around one rigid nipple, then the other.

"Take me back to bed," she demanded in a husky voice.

"Done," he said, standing up with her in his arms and moving around the desk toward the hallway. "Tell me the rest of the plan."

"We drive."

"Where to? North or south?" he asked, running his lips along the column of her throat, his tongue occasionally darting out to lick her skin, making goose bumps spring up all over her body, which was sensitive and primed, slick and ready.

"It doesn't matter . . ." she moaned, threading her hands through his hair as he walked through his bedroom door. He placed her gently on the bed, unwrapping the rest of her body like a present before cutting his eyes to hers. The tenderness she found in his steady gaze was a living, growing thing of such beauty, her heart tripled in size, and all of it—every last inch of space—belonged to him. ". . . as long as I'm sitting beside you."

Chapter 11

In the end, they decided to drive north, and by the time they left the English family penthouse apartment, on December twenty-sixth, with four suitcases full of clothes and personal items, in addition to three boxes crammed with Tom's books and papers, they were feeling more hopeful about their future . . . thanks, in large part, however inadvertently, to Van.

Curled up next to him in the passenger seat, covered with a blanket and snoring softly, Eleanora caught up on sleep as Tom sat in holiday traffic on the Garden State Parkway, headed north to Cornwall, Connecticut. After taking a nice, long look at his gorgeous wife, he turned his eyes to the bumper-to-bumper traffic and his thoughts to his conversation with Van last night.

In the late afternoon, Tom and Eleanora had grudgingly decided to take a break from sex in favor of refueling via breakfast casserole. Sitting on the couch—she in one of his light-blue dress shirts, which fell to her knees, and he in some drawstring pajama pants—with full plates on their laps, they were startled by the ringing phone.

Placing his food on the coffee table, which still bore his little cake, now partially eaten, he picked up the phone on the end table, wondering who was calling on Christmas Day when he was estranged from his family.

His mother? Surely not. She was living in West Palm Beach last he heard, on husband number five or six, but wed, for all intents and purposes, to a bottle of whatever gin was her current favorite.

His little brother? Unlikely. Skip would be at Grandfather's house, and no doubt the favored grandson this holiday, Tom thought ruefully.

And his father had made it clear this morning that he wasn't impressed with Tom's current situation.

Genuinely curious, he put the receiver to his ear. "Hello?"

"Tom? Tom English?"

A giddy female voice on the edge of giggles blasted through the phone, and Tom looked askance at Eleanora, feeling uneasy. He didn't recognize the voice. Was she someone with whom he'd been intimate recently?

He made sure his tone was uninterested. "Ahem. Yes, this is Tom English."

"Don't you know who this is?"

His heart sped up as Eleanora turned to him with curious eyes. "Uhhhh . . ."

"It's Evie!"

"Evie?"

"Yes! Oh my God! Do you remember me?"

His shoulders relaxed, a relieved smile spreading over his face as Eleanora shoved her plate onto the coffee table and practically leaped across the couch for the phone.

Holding it just out of her reach, he answered, "Uh, yeah. I just met you last week."

"That's right! Doesn't it feel like longer? Merry Christmas! Oh my God! How are you? How is Ellie?"

Right now, "Ellie" was straddling his lap, practically wrestling him for the phone, which made her shirt ride up to her hips, giving him a peek at her white underwear. Loving this impromptu wrestling match, he leaned back as far as he could while fending off his wife with one hand.

"She's in the bathroom. She's been in there forever. She might be living there now. I don't even—"

Eleanora gasped, her mouth dropping open, and he launched into silent laughter, weakening his hold on both her and the phone, which she used to her advantage. Straddling his hips and pressed intimately against his body, she reached for the phone and finally grabbed it, shoving it against her ear and scowling at him.

But she didn't move.

She stayed where she was on his lap, and that was, hands down, Tom's favorite thing of all.

"Evie?" she asked, her voice breathless. She gave him a very saucy look, her blue eyes leveling his world, per usual. Then, sticking out her tongue at him, she declared, "No, I'm not constipated, but yes, my husband is an ass."

Tom put on a sad face, watching with delight as her lips twitched into a grin.

"No, I'm not divorcing him. I decided to keep him for a little while."

Tom could hear Evie's shrieks through the phone, and he smiled at his minx of a wife, trailing his hand up and down the smooth softness of her leg until she slapped his hand away.

"He's growing on me."

Suddenly, her expression sobered, and she bit her bottom lip before releasing it.

"Yeah," she murmured, looking away from Tom. "I am."

And it was that "Yeah, I am" that made Tom's brain start racing in an attempt to catch up with his heart. What had Evie just asked her? And what had Eleanora grudgingly admitted to in such a soft and emotional voice? With lightning speed, his mind returned to last night—to the feelings he'd had as he held her, after making love. That was the moment he'd known that he was falling in love with her. And he wondered, could that have been the question Evie asked: *Are you in love with Tom?* And—God, please—could the answer have been, *Yeah, I am*?

He gently stroked her blonde hair from her forehead, and she looked at him again, her eyes soft and searching as she listened to her cousin but scanned his face intently. Suddenly, it was clear that she was refocusing on the phone conversation, and she furrowed her brows.

"Wait. Wait. I missed that. What did you just say?"

She drew her bottom lip into her mouth.

"Evie, what are you talking about? You can't just—"

Tom mouthed *What?* but Eleanora shook her head, her face troubled.

"Honey, let's talk about this a little more. You've never been out of Colorado. Why don't I fly back, and we can—"

Her face tightened as Eve Marie took over the conversation, and finally, Eleanora huffed softly. "I know I'm not your *mother*, but I'm the closest thing you have to a—"

Cupping her cheek, Tom made her look up at him, but she shrugged away, crawling off his lap to kneel on the couch beside him.

"Evie, listen to me. You're *not* going." A slight pause, and then, "No. I'm worried about you! There's a difference!"

Tom reached for Eleanora, placing his palm on her back, but she leaned away from him, resting her elbow on the back of the couch and bowing her head.

"Fine," she said in a broken voice. "Have fun." A long moment passed before she added, "I love you too."

Keeping her back to him, she reached her hand back with the phone and said, "Van wants to talk to you." Then she got up without looking at Tom and padded out of the room, sniffling like she was crying.

Torn between running after Eleanora and talking to Van, Tom pressed the phone to his ear. "Van?"

"Tommy boy! How's married life?"

"It's good. Or, it *was* good until my wife just left the room in tears. What's going on? What just happened?"

"She's crying? Why's she *crying*?"

"How about *you* tell me?" he said, clenching his jaw and curling his fist in his lap, hating like hell that something had upset her.

"Calm down, Tom. It's not a bad thing. You remember my dad's partner? Troy Holmes?"

"Sure."

"Well, he's married now. Has three little kids, in fact. And my dad's sending him over to Hong Kong to open a new office in January. He's leaving from Philly next week."

Tom nodded, wondering what the hell Mr. Van Nostrand's business partner had to do with Eleanora crying in his bathroom. He stood up, looking down the empty hallway, but bound to the living room by the phone's curly cord. "Yeah. And . . . ?"

"Well, Father's asked me to join Troy."

"Okay."

"And, well, Troy's nanny got cold feet about moving to Hong Kong at the last minute, and he asked if I knew any nice girls who could be a nanny to the kids and a friend to Joan, and I suggested—"

"Christ! You didn't!"

"She's a nice person!"

"Eve Marie? She's spread her legs for half of Vail. You're going to pass her off as a nanny?"

Van's voice was like ice. "She's changed."

"In six days?" scoffed Tom. "People don't change that fast."

"Right," said Van, sarcasm heavy in his tone. "Like that would be impossible. Um, you weren't fucking *married* a week ago, hypocrite."

Tom was silent. Van had a point.

"People *can* change that fast," continued Van. "In fact, believe it or not, she and I still haven't . . . haven't actually . . . Tom, if you ever share this with anyone, I will call you a fucking liar."

"Just spit it out, Van."

"We haven't sealed the deal yet."

Tom's mouth dropped open.

"*What?*"

"Don't give me shit, huh? She's . . . I don't know what she is. She's under my goddamned skin is what she is. When Troy told me he needed a nanny, I practically fell to my knees in thanks because I had a reason to invite her along. And yes, I spent the afternoon explaining that Hong Kong wasn't the fictional place where Godzilla was born, but I didn't mind. I don't know what it is about this girl, but she makes me laugh, she makes me feel good. She's just . . ."

"You love her," Tom whispered.

"I don't know about *that*," cried Van. "I just . . . I just don't want to . . . I don't know. I like her a lot. I like her a lot more than a lot. I'm not ready to end this weird thing with her. Not yet."

"So you're going to Hong Kong together."

Van chuckled. "Yep. That's the plan. We leave a week from today. In fact, we're flying back to Philly tomorrow. We were hoping to see you and Ellie while we're in town."

Eleanora walked back into the room with a red nose and bloodshot eyes, and Tom reached for her, relieved when she sank into his lap and curled up in his arms with her cheek on his shoulder and her sweet breath blessing the skin of his throat.

While she leaned on him, Tom told Van about everything that had happened with his grandfather—how he'd soundly rejected Tom's marriage, how Tom had told him to go to hell, how Tom had refused to divorce Eleanora, how they were being kicked out of the penthouse, and how he was about to be blackballed at every financial company on the East Coast.

"So where are you going to go?" asked Van.

"No clue. I have to find work somewhere."

"Let me loan you some—"

"No way, Van," said Tom, using his free hand to stroke Eleanora's back. "I have some savings. We'll be okay."

"Hey!" said Van. "Wait a second! I have an idea!"

Tom heard papers rustling in the background and used the free moment to whisper in Eleanora's ear. "Van cares about her, baby. He'll look after her in Hong Kong."

He felt her clench her jaw against his collarbone and decided to leave it alone for now.

Van came back on the line. "Listen, my folks had Juanita forward my mail to Vail, and . . . yeah, here it is. The alumni bulletin from Kinsey Hall. Do you remember Professor Wiggins?"

"Wacky Wigs?" asked Tom, a brief smile stretching his lips as he recalled the elderly teacher at the Connecticut boarding school where he and Van had first met each other. "Sure. Freshman and sophomore English, right?"

"Right. He was eighty-two. He passed away last month."

"Aw," said Tom, feeling a genuine sense of sadness. "That's too bad."

"Yeah. It's sad," said Van. "But they still haven't found a replacement."

"For . . ."

"Freshman and sophomore English," said Van. "The parents are starting to complain because they've gone through three subs since Thanksgiving break. Why don't you—"

"What? Teach?"

"Sure, teach. Teach at Kinsey. You're an alum, Tom. You went to Princeton. They'd be crazy to turn you away."

"Van, I know *nothing* about teaching kids."

"That might be true, dummy, and *I* know that, and *you* know that, but you know who doesn't know that? The dean of Kinsey Hall."

Tom talked to Van for a few more minutes, then urged Eleanora to patch things up with her cousin before hanging up. By the time she got off the phone, she was still weepy, but she managed to smile for him as they said good-bye.

"Lots of postcards," said Eleanora. "And letters! I mean it, Evie! A letter a week." A pause. "I don't care. I'll buy you a dictionary, and you can look up the ones you don't know." Another pause. "I wouldn't have . . . I might not have left Romero without you. I know. I love you too. Be safe."

Tom hung up the phone and let Eleanora cry on his shoulder for a good twenty minutes before he finally calmed her down and convinced her that her cousin would be fine.

"It's just so far away."

It was on the tip of Tom's tongue to tell her that they'd go visit Eve Marie whenever she wanted to, and it stung to realize he couldn't make her that sort of promise anymore. He could no longer afford that sort of luxury.

"My whole life has just changed so fast," she sobbed. "Meeting you. Getting married. Leaving Colorado. Now leaving Philadelphia. It's a lot."

He held her closer, pressing his lips to her temple. "You're tough, baby."

"I don't feel tough, Tom."

"You are," he said, leaning back and running his fingers through her hair. "You're exceptional. And you're mine. And we're going to make it. In fact . . ."

His voice faded in his head as he merged onto the Palisades Parkway. He'd shared Van's idea with her, watching her face morph from grieved cousin to supportive spouse in a matter of minutes. She declared it a wonderful idea and asked him a battery of questions about Kinsey Hall and Connecticut, her eyes sparkling with enthusiasm and hope.

"I'll call them tomorrow," he promised her.

"Nope," she said, sitting up straight on his lap, her hands pressed down on his shoulders like she meant business. "We'll leave early tomorrow, and you'll go *see* them. Make your case in person, Tom. Get the job. You can do this!"

"Yeah?" he asked, marveling at her go-getter spirit and seeing, so clearly, the young girl who'd left her small town to find a better life in Vail.

He remembered some musings he'd had while they were in Vegas—wondering if there was anything she couldn't do, wondering if she could be born in a poor town in Colorado and end up a millionaire's wife. Or, heck, maybe a teacher's wife. And the most incredible, wonderful thing about Eleanora Watters English? The fact that though his salary—if he even *got* the job—would likely keep them just on the outskirts of comfortable, it wouldn't bother her. She'd roll with it. She'd make it work.

It made his heart swell and surge with love for her. For her spirit and hope, for her faith in him, for her unsinkable, unshakable, unwavering conviction that things could always be worked out, that life could always be better.

"Yeah," she said, beaming at him, her eyes bright and alive.

"I'm falling in love with you," he murmured. "I can't help it. When life presents you someone between a dream and a miracle, you hold on as tight as you can."

Her eyes flooded with tears, but instead of answering his declaration with one of her own, she clasped his face fiercely in her trembling hands and kissed him passionately, letting him cradle her in his arms and carry her back to bed.

Sighing happily, he glanced over again at her sleeping form in the passenger seat and debated whether to wake her up. She'd told him that she wanted to see the views from the Bear Mountain Bridge, but he was reluctant to interrupt her rest after he'd kept her up for two nights straight.

Just as he paid the toll to cross the Hudson River, her eyes fluttered open, and she looked up at him with a lazy smile that made his heart jump.

"Hello, husband," she murmured.

My heart.

"Hello, wife," he answered, his voice gravelly.

She grinned at him, her blue eyes a mirror of yet-unspoken love.

"Are we there yet?"

Chapter 12

"Dean Gordon," said Tom, smiling at the older gentleman and offering his hand in greeting.

"Well, Tom English, you're a sight for sore eyes."

He pumped Tom's hand in the doorway of his office, then put his arm around Tom's shoulders, ushering him into the one-hundred-fifty-year-old head dean's office at Kinsey Hall.

"Yes, sir. Thank you, sir."

Tom had graduated from Kinsey fourteen years ago, but finding himself face-to-face with the former assistant dean, he couldn't help feeling like a student again.

"Ha, ha," chortled Neville Gordon, slapping Tom on the back. "They all come back and still call me sir." He gestured to a rich-looking leather sofa. "Take a seat."

"Thank you, sir."

"Neville, Tom!" said Dean Gordon, taking a seat behind his desk. "We're peers now. Neville's just fine."

"Thank you for taking the time to see me, um, Neville," said Tom, smoothing his white shirtfront with his palm.

It turned out that Eleanora was not very handy with an iron. She had scorched one of his shirts on the ironing board in their room at the Howard Johnson's Motor Lodge before Tom took over the job. However, Tom had never ironed a shirt either and soon understood how she'd scorched the first. The third shirt was at least wearable since the tan iron imprint was on the back, covered by his suit jacket.

"Don't want to rush you, son, but my daughter—do you remember Charity?—is coming to meet me for lunch. She just broke off her engagement with another Kinsey alum, Geoffrey Atwell, though her mother and I are hoping she'll patch it up." He sighed, realizing he'd digressed. "What can I do for you, Tom?"

Tom hid a small, quasi-unkind grin. He did remember both Charity and Geoffrey. Geoffrey had been his year. And Charity had been, ahem, popular.

"Yes, well, I'll get to the point. I heard the sad news about Professor Wiggins."

"Ah, yes. Poor Wigs. Did you know he was my teacher too? And your father's," added Dean Gordon, his voice cooling a little at the mention of Tom's father. "Everyone thought Franklin Wiggins would outlast Kinsey. But cancer's a friend to no man."

"No, sir," said Tom.

Dean Gordon sighed. "He lived a good life. Taught for sixty years, Tom. How do you like that?"

"Impressive, sir."

"I'll say. Hard to replace. Having a devil of a time."

Tom's eyes widened. "Well, sir, that's actually why I'm here."

"Come again?" asked Dean Gordon, looking up, distracted from his thoughts of his fallen colleague.

"The vacancy in the English department. I'd like to fill it."

Dean Gordon narrowed his eyes, evaluating Tom. "You would, would you? Have a lot of teaching experience, Tom?"

Tom thought about lying. Truly, he did. But he wasn't a very good liar. He didn't like having to remember his lies, and besides, Dean Gordon had always been kind to Tom. He deserved honesty.

"Not a bit, sir."

Dean Gordon chortled as though Tom was making a joke, then sobered as Tom stared back at him plain faced. "Oh, I see."

"I worked for English & Son until a week ago."

"English & Son. With your father. And grandfather."

Was it Tom's imagination, or did Dean Gordon's voice cool again?

"Yes, sir."

"But no longer."

Tom sighed. In for a penny, in for a pound. "No, sir. I recently got married, and my grandfather doesn't . . ." He lifted his chin in defiance. "That is, he doesn't approve of my wife, sir. I've been cut off."

Neville Gordon's eyes widened and he sat back in his chair, tenting his fingers. "Is that so?"

"Yes, sir. That's the truth."

"Blackballed too, I presume?"

Tom nodded, swallowing the bile in his throat. "Yes, sir."

Dean Gordon nodded slowly, staring at Tom with compassion. "I knew your grandfather a little."

"Sir?"

"I was your father's *original* roommate, but I was first-generation Kinsey, here on scholarship, and your father, Bertram, was the fifth English to attend. At your grandfather's request, we were switched around."

Tom ground his teeth. How fucking embarrassing.

"I'm sorry, Dean Gordon. He's . . ."

". . . set in his ways," said Dean Gordon quickly, before Tom could say something worse. "I never blamed your father, Tom. Bertram was a good sort of fellow. Affable. Friend to everyone."

"Weak," snarled Tom softly.

"He wasn't unkind to me." Dean Gordon paused. "Though he never met a battle more important than keeping the peace, I'll give you that."

Tom rubbed his hand on the slick leather of the couch arm, sitting forward. "I'm sorry I came here. I'm not qualified to teach, and my family—"

"Tom, you went to Princeton. You studied . . . ?"

"English, sir."

"English." Dean Gordon smiled. "We *are* looking for an English teacher. Let's say I hired you . . . at least until the end of the year. That's six months. What would you teach in six months to an unruly group of fourteen- and fifteen-year-olds, eh, Tom?"

For the next twenty minutes, Tom talked about his favorite novels, short stories, and poems. He told the dean that although he'd respected Professor Wiggins, the old teacher had preferred classical literature and hadn't discussed the contemporary writers—Vonnegut, Bradbury, King—whom Tom would have liked to share with the boys.

"*Stephen* King?"

"His novellas are excellent, sir."

Finally, Dean Gordon sighed, gently slapping his desk twice and nodding at Tom. "Truly think you're up to it? Six weeks of novels, six weeks of short stories, and six weeks of poetry? Not much time to get up to speed. Can you come up with a curriculum by next week, when the boys come back from Christmas break?"

Tom's heart beat faster as he realized that Dean Gordon was actually—unbelievably—giving him a chance.

"I'll give it my best, sir. I can promise enthusiasm!"

"Salary's not much, Tom," he said, his eyes sorry. "Seventeen thousand annual, and I can't offer you health care until next year."

Seventeen thousand dollars and no benefits?

Tom kept himself from wincing. He had only five thousand dollars in his bank account to begin with. Well, they'd just have to make it last.

"Could I pick up some extra work, if needed?"

"I don't suppose you want to stay in the dorms as a resident adviser when you have a pretty, young wife at home?"

Then Tom *did* wince.

Dean Gordon chuckled. "There's always tutoring, son."

"I'll make it work, sir."

Dean Gordon stood up, extending his hand. "Me too. I'll need your semester syllabus for approval on January second. Boys come back the Monday after. Deal?"

"Yes! Yes, sir."

"Well, welcome back to Kinsey, Tom."

Tom leaped up and shook the dean's hand, beaming at his new boss. "Thank you. I just . . . I can't wait to tell . . . Thank you!"

"What's her name? Your bride?"

"Eleanora, sir."

"Eleanora English, eh? The girl who made Tom defy old Theodore. I'm fond of her already."

"Me too, sir," said Tom, chuckling softly.

"Neville, son. We're colleagues now."

The door to the office opened suddenly, and Tom dropped Dean Gordon's hand, turning to find a pretty, young blonde woman standing in the doorway of her father's office: Charity Gordon. He would have known her anywhere.

"Ah, Charity!" said her father, circling the desk to greet his daughter with a quick kiss on the cheek.

But Charity barely acknowledged her father. She only had eyes for Tom. Big, wide, dark eyes for Tom, and lips that she suddenly felt the need to wet slowly and with great to-do before letting them tip into a sexy grin.

"Tom? Tom English?"

"Charity," he said, stepping forward and holding out his hand. "You look well."

She ignored his hand, enveloping him in a Chanel-scented hug that pressed her large breasts against the shirt his wife had tried to help him iron an hour ago. He patted Charity's back awkwardly, wishing she'd let go of him. Finally, she did, though she barely moved far enough away for them to keep from touching.

"Tom English, as I live and breathe. You look . . ." She swept her eyes down his body and then back up slowly. ". . . fine."

Dean Gordon had been putting on his overcoat as Tom and Charity exchanged pleasantries, but now he turned and smiled at them both.

"I've just hired Tom!"

Charity gasped, pressing her hand to her chest. "No!"

"Yes, dearest, it's true. Tom is our new English teacher."

She laughed softly. "But didn't I hear that you were a banker, Tom? Something delicious like that?"

"I've decided to give teaching a try," he said.

"Slumming in the country for a few months?" she asked, a teasing twinkle in her bright, blue eyes. "Like community service?"

"Come now, dearest," said her father. "That isn't seemly."

She gave her father a bored look and turned back to Tom with a brilliant smile. "Be serious now: are you *really* teaching here?"

"I've said so. Yes."

"Well." She shrugged. "That'll make the long winter less lonely. How about we have some fun while we're both stranded in the middle of nowhere, eh?"

"That's a jolly good idea," agreed Dean Gordon, grinning at Tom. "Why don't you and your new wife join us for dinner next week, eh?"

"Wife?" asked Charity, her expression frosting over. "You're . . . married?"

Tom nodded, holding up his ring finger, which wore the simple, gold band Eleanora had slid on his finger in Vegas. "Newly."

"Oh," she said, taking a deep breath and giving him a much tighter smile than the enthusiastic ones she'd showered on him before. "Well, congratulations, I guess."

"Thanks, I guess," he said.

"I've just broken my engagement," she said, as though engagements—and maybe even new marriages—were made to be broken.

"Yes, I heard. To Geoffrey Atwell." Tom wasn't sure of the protocol when someone announced their broken engagement without a hint of sorrow. "Too bad. Decent guy, Atwell."

"That's what *we've* been trying to tell her!" said Dean Gordon.

Charity rolled her eyes at both men, pulling on her black, leather gloves and sighing. "Geoffrey Atwell will still be waiting if I change my mind, Daddy. There's no rush."

He doubted Atwell felt the same, but Tom hid his true feelings with a grim smile, turning away from Charity and facing Dean Gordon. "Sir, I'll see you next week."

Neville Gordon smiled at Tom, ushering his daughter out of the office and flicking the lights off before saying, "I meant it about dinner, Tom. New Year's, eh? Come for dinner on New Year's Day, won't you?"

"Yes," agreed Charity with barely concealed machinations narrowing her eyes. "Come for New Year's. And bring the little woman too."

While Tom had gone to Kinsey Hall to interview for a job, he'd tasked Eleanora with trying to find an apartment for them somewhere in or around Cornwall. But the small towns around Cornwall—Weston, Sharon, New Preston, Kent, and Warren—didn't have many apartments for rent; they had houses. And most of the houses in these quiet, little towns were asking almost a thousand dollars per month for rent. The problem with this—aside from the fact that it was highway robbery—was that paying up the first and last months' rent and security deposit would leave Tom only two thousand dollars in savings. Even with her saved eight hundred dollars thrown into the mix, it simply wasn't much to live on.

"What do you think, Mrs. English?" asked the real estate agent, Gladys Hoover, who was kind, but clearly had other things she'd rather be doing two days after Christmas.

"It's lovely," said Eleanora, looking around the living room of a three-bedroom house that was way too big for her and Tom. "But nine-fifty a month is just too much."

Gladys huffed impatiently. "My son's having a holiday do in an hour. I don't suppose we could look at more tomorrow?"

"I promised my husband that I'd—"

"Very well, Mrs. English. We'll go see another. Fair warning, this next one is absurdly small. Still," she flicked a glance over Eleanora's threadbare, out-of-date coat, "maybe it will do."

Eleanora got into Gladys's Cadillac and, grateful that they were all small-talked out, looked out the window at the rolling hills of Connecticut, covered in pristine white.

It was a beautiful place, if somewhat stark, though Tom had assured her as they drove into town that it was peerless in springtime. He'd even recited a poem for her just before they turned into the parking lot of the Howard Johnson's:

So when the earth is alive with gods,
And the lusty ploughman breaks the sod,
And the grass sings in the meadows,
And the flowers smile in the shadows,
Sits my heart at ease,
Hearing the song of the leas,
Singing the songs of the meadows.

"Who wrote that?" she asked, grinning at him with delight. "You?"

"No, sunshine," he'd replied. "Robert Louis Stevenson, though it's sometimes credited to D. H. Lawrence."

"Do I know anything he wrote?"

Tom chuckled softly. "Lawrence? He wrote a very naughty book called *Lady Chatterley's Lover*."

"How naughty?"

"*Very.*"

"Tell me some of it."

"How about I *read* you some of it?"

"Tonight?" she'd asked.

"Tomorrow night," he'd bargained. "I'll have to dig through the boxes to find it. And anyway, wife, you need some sleep tonight."

He'd made love to her only once last night in their motel-room bed, and the rhythm of their bodies moving together echoed in the squeak of the box spring.

"Well, this is romantic," he commented at one point, and they both started laughing, despite the fact that he was deeply embedded inside her. Somehow their giggles turned to happy kisses to heat to now to more to yes, and suddenly, she didn't hear the squeaks at all. She heard only his breath against her neck, the pounding of her heart in her head, and felt the clenching and writhing and stream of liquid heat on her skin as he pulled out of her at the last moment and came beneath her breasts.

She would never get enough of him. Never.

"Here we are," chirped Gladys. "The smallest house in Weston."

Eleanora looked up at a small, white house, neat and tidy, with a front porch big enough for two rockers. An expanse of white fields spread out behind the house, with nothing troubling her view of the Berkshire Hills beyond. Windows flanked a black-painted door, whose brass knocker glistened like gold in the light of the setting sun. The house smiled at her in its own way, and she smiled back, thinking, *I'm home.*

"We'll take it," she murmured.

"You haven't even seen it yet," protested Gladys.

"How much is it?" asked Eleanora without glancing away from her house.

"Six hundred a month."

"We'll take it," she said again.

Meeting her back at the hotel late that afternoon, after spending some time at the local library, Tom shared the good news that he was the newest faculty member of Kinsey Hall, and Eleanora shared the good news that they now had a six-month lease on a tiny house in nearby Weston.

They celebrated by having dinner in the motel restaurant and splitting a hot fudge sundae before trudging back through the snow to their room. Once inside, Tom turned up the heat and produced a shabby paperback from his jacket pocket.

"That," said Eleanora, toeing off her boots and hanging her coat in the closet, "looks like a *very* naughty book."

Tom fairly hummed with anticipation. "It is."

Despite the fact that he'd be bringing home only about a thousand dollars a month after taxes, he felt buoyant tonight—excited, even—as he faced the prospect of a life with Eleanora. She was resourceful and plucky, supportive and enthusiastic, and he would work as hard as he needed to, to keep her happy . . . starting with a memorable fucking orgasm tonight, after introducing her to D. H. Lawrence's insanely erotic novel, *Lady Chatterley's Lover*.

"So?" she asked, turning around and giving him a slow, saucy look. "Do you want me to sit on the bed while you read? Or . . . ?"

"I was thinking we could read back and forth," he said. "And while one person reads, the other . . . strips."

"Inventive. Strip reading instead of strip poker."

He grinned at her, shrugging out of his overcoat and taking off his boots. "Now we're even."

She sat down on the bed, looking up at him. "Start reading."

Tom opened the old book, turning to one of several dog-eared pages to comply with her demand.

"*His body was urgent against her, and she hadn't the heart any more to fight . . . She saw his eyes, tense and brilliant, fierce, not loving. But her will had left her. A strange weight was on her limbs. She was giving way,*" read Tom, his eyes flicking up near constantly to watch his wife slowly, so slowly, pull her sweater over her blonde hair and drop it on the floor.

She reached out her hand for the book. He handed it to her, pointing to where he'd left off.

"*She was giving up . . . she had to lie down there under the boughs of the tree, like an animal, while he waited, standing there in his shirt and breeches, watching her with haunted eyes . . . He too had bared the front part of his body and she felt his naked flesh against her as he came into her. For a moment he was still inside her, turgid there and quivering,*" she finished, her voice lower and more gravelly than it had been when she started.

Tom's sweater lay on top of hers.

"Your turn," she said.

He took the book, watching her as he recited from memory, "*Then as he began to move, in the sudden helpless orgasm, there awoke in her new strange thrills rippling inside her. Rippling, rippling, rippling, like a flapping overlapping of soft flames, soft as feathers, running to points of brilliance, exquisite, exquisite and melting her all molten inside.*"

Eleanora's turtleneck shirt joined their sweaters on the floor, and Tom dropped his eyes to her breasts, watching as her nipples puckered, pushing against the material of her bra, straining and hard. His blood surged, and his cock swelled behind his jeans.

"You have it memorized?" she asked, holding his eyes.

"We weren't allowed to have porn at Kinsey. This was the closest we could get."

"So you all read it a million times."

"A million or more," he said, holding out the book to her, "dreaming about a girl like you."

She licked her lips and took the book from him, reading, "*It was like bells rippling up and up to a culmination. She lay unconscious of the wild little cries she uttered at the last. But it was over too soon, too soon, and she could no longer force her own conclusion with her own activity. This was different, different. She could do nothing. She could no longer harden and grip for her own satisfaction upon him. She could only wait, wait and moan in spirit as she felt him withdrawing, withdrawing and contracting, coming to the terrible moment when he would slip out of her and be gone.*"

He tore his turtleneck over his head, glad that his T-shirt hitched a ride, baring his chest to her.

"This is," she said, raising her eyes to his, her breathing shallow and audible, "hot."

"I told you," he said.

She dropped her gaze to his bare chest, then quickly reached behind and unfastened her bra. "New rule: two pieces of clothing each time."

"Whatever you want, baby," he said.

"I want you to read," she murmured, handing him the book as her bra whispered down her arms and slipped to the growing pile of clothes on the floor.

Tom's mouth watered, and he had to swallow before dropping his eyes to the text. He took a shaky breath, feeling his cock twitch as she unbuttoned and unzipped her jeans.

"Read, Tom," she said, pushing the denim over her hips.

"*Whilst all her womb was open and soft, and softly clamouring, like a sea-anemone under the tide, clamouring for him to come in again and make a fulfilment for her. She clung to him unconscious in passion, and he never quite slipped from her, and she felt the soft bud of him within her stirring, and strange rhythms flushing up into her with a strange rhythmic growing motion, swelling and swelling till it filled all her cleaving consciousness . . .*"

He looked up, and she was lying naked on the bed, her head braced up on one elbow so that she could watch him.

"Jesus," he murmured, clenching his jaw. She was every teenage boy's—every man's—erotic fantasy come true. And she was his.

She grinned at him like she could read his mind, then licked her lips, holding out her hand. "Give it to me, husband, and finish stripping."

He placed the book on the bed beside her, then reached for his belt buckle.

Her voice, dulcet and low, thick with passion, picked up where he left off, ". . . *and then began again the unspeakable motion that was not really motion, but pure deepening whirlpools of sensation swirling deeper and deeper through all her tissue and consciousness, till she was one perfect concentric fluid of feeling, and she lay there crying in unconscious inarticulate cries.*"

She had flipped to her back while reading, drawing her knees up and open, and now Tom knelt between them, his cock standing tall and proud, pulsing and twitching with arousal. He cut his eyes to hers and found them dark and drugged, soft and waiting.

"Make me cry in unconscious, inarticulate cries, Tom," she said, her lips tilting into a sexy grin as she stared up at him.

This girl.

This woman.

His woman.

How she embraced life. How she rolled with its punches, forever leaning into it and never away. In such a short time, she had become his coconspirator and helpmate, his cheerleader and lover. His friend. His partner. His wife. His . . . beloved.

"Eleanora," he said, savoring her name against his lips as he positioned the tip of his sex at the entrance of hers.

"Mmm?"

"I love you," he said, surging forward to merge his body with hers.

Her lips parted in surprise—half from his unexpected admission and half from the perfection of their joining—and she gasped, her eyes fluttering closed as he pushed forward. When he was fully sheathed within her, his pelvis flush with hers, she opened them again. They sparkled like sapphires, shining brightly amid an ocean of unshed tears.

"Tom," she whispered, reaching for his face and pulling him down to her. "I love you too."

He kissed her madly, rocking into her, faster and faster, promising her with his body that his words were true.

Her cries and moans overtook the squeaking of their motel room bed, the walls of her sex tightening around him, pulsing in waves, until he could barely endure the sweetness. He forced himself to withdraw at the last possible moment to spend himself on her belly.

And then he clutched her to his body, the heat of their lovemaking binding them flesh to flesh, the power of their new love binding them heart to heart.

Chapter 13

Eleanora had worked every New Year's Eve since she was fourteen years old, slinging pitchers of beer at a bar in Romero and, once she'd gotten to Vail, working the all-night shift at Auntie Rose's because she hoped the tips would be good. And they were—last year's New Year's Eve tips had paid her rent through February.

She'd never had someone special with whom to celebrate New Year's, no one to dress up for, no one she'd want to kiss at midnight. The couple of no-account boys she'd dated in high school hadn't been worth losing her tips for, and she'd worked too hard, between Auntie Rose's and community college, to date anyone seriously in Vail.

So this year was new territory for Eleanora: for the first time in her adult life, she was going to celebrate New Year's Eve, *and* she had someone special to kiss at midnight. And she greeted the holiday with excitement and anticipation.

Tom had been spending every day at the Weston Memorial Library. Eleanora dropped him off at ten o'clock so she would have the car all day and picked him up when the library closed, at five. He was creating the syllabus for the freshman and sophomore English classes he would be teaching, rereading books and stories to gauge their appropriateness, and coming up with study plans. Every evening, as they ate breakfast-for-dinner, he'd tell her about his progress, and she'd listen with enthusiasm and approval, before telling him which parts of their little house she'd scrubbed clean and what frugal purchases she'd made to feather their modest nest.

But today, New Year's Eve, she wouldn't just drop him off at the library before heading home. No. Today Eleanora Watters English was on a mission, and it required her sneaking into the library after dropping Tom off and somehow evading him as she hunted her quarry.

"I love you tons," he said tenderly, leaning over the car bolster to kiss her good-bye, as he did every morning.

Her toes curled as he kissed her. Heat, never absent for long, pooled in her belly. "I love you back."

"See you at five?"

She nodded, grinning at him. "I'll be here. And no flirting with the librarians."

He picked up his satchel off the floor and winked at her. "Didn't you ever hear what Paul Newman said about philandering?"

"Educate me."

"He said, and I quote, 'I have steak at home. Why should I go out for hamburger?'"

She chuckled. "Did you just compare me to meat?"

"You're filet mignon, baby."

"You better believe it," she said, grabbing his neck for one more kiss before letting him go.

He hopped up the steps of the library, but just before stepping inside, he turned around and grinned at her, pursing his lips into one more quick kiss before disappearing inside.

Eleanora sighed happily, pulling away from the curb in front of the little brick building and circling the block. When she approached the building again, she pulled into the rear parking lot and cut the engine.

She took off her coat and threw it in the back seat, then pulled on an old, brown sweater and tied a scarf around her hair. Donning Jackie O–style sunglasses she'd picked up at a pharmacy in Vail, she checked her reflection in the rearview mirror before heading into the library via the back door.

Walking with her head down, she desperately hoped that she wouldn't run into Tom and ruin the surprise. After a week of breakfast for every meal, she was going to make dinner tonight. A *real* dinner.

The problem? She had no idea how. Her mission was to find a cookbook, check it out of the library, choose a recipe in the car, and head straight to the Davis IGA to get everything she needed. When she left to pick up Tom, she planned to have the table set, an elegant dinner warming in the oven, and chilled white wine ready to be enjoyed the moment they arrived home.

After all, it felt like the least she could do. Tom was working so hard for both of them, having insisted that he wanted to support her. She would use her savings to treat him to a little celebration tonight. Besides, they'd been married for exactly ten days today, and if that wasn't something to celebrate, Eleanora couldn't think of anything that was.

Sliding into the first row of books she saw, she peeked through two stacks and found Tom sitting at a table not far from her. He had his back to her and his shoulders hunched forward as though reading. His blond hair was shiny from the sun billowing in through the windows in front of him and a little long in the back, she noticed, the waved edges brushing the collar of the crisp, blue shirt that she'd successfully ironed for him this morning. Her fingers twitched because they knew so well the feel of those strands threaded between her digits. Soft and downy and—

"Tom! Is this where you've been hiding?"

Eleanora jolted forward against the stack of books before her, watching as a tall, classy, blonde woman wearing a black cashmere coat and holding a black fur muff sidled up to her husband's table.

Moving as stealthily as possible, Eleanora slipped to the end of one stack of books and inserted herself into the next, now concealed by only one stack as she spied on her husband. She lowered her sunglasses as the woman sat down on the edge of the table, her coat falling open to reveal long legs and high-heeled shoes.

Tom half stood, but the woman placed her hand on his shoulder familiarly and pushed him back into his chair.

"My view from up here is smashing," she gushed, giggling. "Don't ruin it by standing up."

Eleanora's eyes narrowed. This woman was pretty. No, she was beautiful. And she was obviously wealthy, judging from her clothes. And she definitely knew Tom.

"Good morning, Charity."

"Good morning, Tom," she said, putting on a deep and serious voice before giggling again. "We have to lighten you up a little!" Her hand, which had lingered on Tom's shoulder, slid down his arm in a caress. "Trouble with the little woman?"

The little woman? Huh! This woman, this Charity, *with whom my husband is so familiar, is talking about* me, she thought, which raised the question, if Charity knew about Eleanora, how come Eleanora didn't know about Charity?

"No," said Tom, who didn't remove Charity's offending hand.

"She *did* get you disowned." Her hand squeezed, and her voice dripped with sympathy. "Poor baby."

Eleanora's face fell. How did this woman know so much about her? About *them*?

"I need to get back to work, Charity."

"You work too hard!" exclaimed Charity, who slipped her hand into Tom's. "Have lunch with me today."

"I can't," he said, looking up at her. "Too much to do."

"All work and no play, Tommy."

Tommy? Jesus! *Tommy?*

Tom cleared his throat, finally taking back his hand to run it through his hair, then folding it with his other hand on his lap.

Eleanora was seething by now, her breath coming in fast, furious draws as she hid behind the tragedies of Shakespeare.

Meanwhile, Charity showed no signs of leaving.

"Can't wait to see you tomorrow," she purred in a low, sexy tone.

Tomorrow? He was seeing her tomorrow? Eleanora held her breath, her chest burning and painful as she waited for his reply.

"Oh, that's right."

"Did you forget?"

"Of course not," he said. "I'll have to, uh—"

"Good! I can't wait," she said, reaching out to tousle his hair. "Know what I was thinking about this morning?"

"Nope," said Tom.

"Remember the time we went skinny-dipping in Weston Falls?"

Eleanora gasped, her arm jerking forward and shoving *Macbeth* right through the stack, which knocked the book behind it to the wood floor a few feet away from Tom's table. Eleanora crouched down as it thudded loudly to the floor. From behind the lower shelf, she saw Tom and Charity look quickly in her direction, but she was concealed behind the lower shelf of books, and they went back to their conversation.

"Remember?" said Charity again, slapping Tom's shoulder playfully.

"Um," he said. "Yeah. Long time ago."

"Not *so* long ago," she said, swinging her leg back and forth.

How *recently*? Eleanora wondered, watching Charity's leg brush against her husband's thigh.

And suddenly, a terrible lump rose in her throat, sidelining her anger and giving rise to fear. Who was she? An ex-girlfriend? For God's sake, the way she was behaving, it seemed more like she was a . . . a . . . *current* girlfriend. Eleanora's heart clutched as her eyes watered painfully.

"Miss? Miss? Did you knock down that book?" Eleanora looked up to find a gray-haired lady contemplating her from the end of the row with bushy, furrowed eyebrows and a deep, disapproving frown. "Are you hiding back here knocking books over?"

"Shhh!" whispered Eleanora, popping up so fast, her elbow caught *King Lear* and *Hamlet*, knocking them to the floor.

"That's it!" said the old librarian, hustling down the row, waggling her finger at Eleanora. "You can't come here and hurt the books!"

"I'm going!" she snarled in a loud whisper, adjusting her askew sunglasses and feeling like a hybrid of an idiot and a chump. "Just stop yelling! Shhhh!"

"You shhh!"

"You shhh!" she whisper-yelled back, making her way quickly back down the row before they drew an audience.

She peeked out between some books at the end of the aisle to see Charity's head thrown back, giggling at something Tom was saying. Taking a deep, ragged breath, Eleanora lifted her chin, took a right toward the exit, and slammed the library door shut behind her as hard as she possibly could.

It has not been a very good day, mused Tom, who trudged home on icy, snow-covered sidewalks in the cold dark.

Oh, it had started off auspicious enough: sunrise sex with his gorgeous, amazing wife, another delicious breakfast, and the sweetest-ever kiss good-bye as she dropped him off at the library this morning. But it had all gone downhill from there.

First of all, Charity Gordon, who couldn't take a hint if the word *hint* was flashing neon in her face, had wasted almost half an hour of his time this morning, bothering him about going out to lunch, reconfirming dinner for tomorrow—which he'd forgotten to mention to his wife— and reminding him of stupid boarding school shenanigans. No, he hadn't gone skinny-dipping with her, he'd wanted to say. *She'd* gone skinny dipping with Geoffrey Atwell and Trent Hughes. Tom and Van had happened upon them and had a good laugh stealing their clothes.

The thing about Charity, however, was that as forward and annoying as she was, she was also Dean Gordon's daughter, and Tom needed to keep things friendly with her father. He needed the job offered to him at Kinsey. So he wasn't anxious to insult Charity by telling her to bug off. But it made him feel funny to be seen in public with Charity, like he was somehow betraying Eleanora, even though the sun rose, set, and shined in his wife's eyes.

Second of all, the librarian—the older, graying lady whom he sometimes found cooing to the books or petting them like kittens—had come over to see him around four fifty-five to say that his wife had called to say the car wouldn't start. He'd need to walk home.

"Walk home?" he asked, sure he'd misunderstood her. It was four or five miles.

"Shhh! It's a library. Lower your voice!" the older lady whisper-yelled. "Yes. Walk. Car won't start."

"Are you sure she called for me?"

"You're Thomas English. I see your library card at the end of every day."

His shoulders had slumped, and he sighed. Not only would he have to walk home with five or six books weighing down his satchel, but it would take over an hour to get there, and he hated waiting that long to see her. Not to mention, they didn't have the money to fix a broken starter, which worried him as he slipped and slid down the frosty New England sidewalks, heading out of the well-lit village.

"Not a very good day at all," he grumbled, thinking about the call he'd made to his father while he took a half-hour break at lunchtime.

He'd used the pay phone in the basement of the library, feeding it dime after dime until his father's apartment phone had rung.

"Hello, Bertram English's residence."

"Flora, it's Tom," he said, greeting his father's maid.

"Mister Tom! Merry Christmas and Happy New Year!"

"To you too. Is my father there?"

"Yes, sir. Hold the line, please."

A moment later, his father picked up. "Tom?"

"Father."

"Have you come to your senses?"

Tom flinched, his nostrils flaring as he took a deep breath to swallow the words he wanted to say—*Fuck you, sir* holding a place of pride at the top of the list.

"If you're asking if I'm still married, I am."

"Tom, be reasonable."

"I just wanted to give you my address."

"We could talk to your grandfather together. We could—"

"If any scenario you have in mind includes me annulling my marriage or divorcing my wife, then we have nothing to discuss."

His father was silent.

"We are living at 33 Stony Brook Road in Weston, Connecticut, near—"

"Kinsey," said his father. "What the hell are you doing all the way up there?"

"I got a job," said Tom, "at Kinsey. Teaching English."

"Teaching!"

"Yes."

"Teaching kids English?"

This time, Tom was silent.

"Well, thanks so much, Thomas. We'll be the laughing-stock of the club when everyone finds out. First you marry some anonymous little slut from Denver, and then you—"

"Shut. Your. Mouth!" bellowed Tom, his spittle covering the mouthpiece of the phone. "You will *not*—I repeat, sir— you will *not* speak about my wife in that manner. I know well your contempt for marriage, as evidenced by your three discarded wives. But you will not talk about mine without respect."

"You're digging a deep grave, Tom," said his father sadly. "Your grandfather regrets how things were left between you. He missed you at Christmas. He's pliant now. If you'd just—"

"I love her," said Tom quietly, owning the words with every breath he drew, every beat of his heart. "I won't give her up."

"Then there's nothing more to say." His father sighed. "Happy New Year, Tom."

"And to you, Father. Good-bye."

He hung up the phone quickly, still shaking from his fury, the words *anonymous little slut* making him see red. All he wanted after that was to leave the library and race home to her, hold her in his arms, smell her wonderful maple syrup smell, and reaffirm that the sort of love he bore her was the kind that would continue to grow and last a lifetime.

Instead, he was walking home through two-foot snowdrifts.

As their little house finally came into sight after a ninety-minute walk, Tom noticed that the house didn't look bright and cheery, but dark and quiet. The front light, which Eleanora always left on, was off.

He pushed his key in the lock and turned the knob, stepping into the living room.

"Eleanora?" he called.

It didn't smell like eggs and hash browns or pancakes and bacon. It didn't smell like anything at all. And though he'd expected Eleanora to race to the door and greet him, his wife was nowhere to be found.

He peeked into the kitchen, flicking on the light. She wasn't there, though there was a foil-covered plate on the table with a taped note on top that read "Dinner."

"Eleanora?" he called again, walking up the stairs to their bedroom on the second floor.

Pushing open the bedroom door, he found the room lit up with the ambient light from the black-and-white, secondhand TV on the dresser. Eleanora sat up in bed, under the covers, staring at the TV.

Tom sat down on the bed beside her. "Hey, baby. Car wouldn't start, huh?"

She didn't look at him, just cleared her throat like he wasn't there and continued to stare at the news.

Tom flinched. "Eleanora?"

"Your dinner's on the table," she said, her voice dull and cold.

He reached for her face, turning her head gently to face him. Even in the dim light, he could tell that her eyes were puffy and sad.

"What's wrong? Are you okay? Baby, you're scaring me."

She jerked her head away, looking back at the TV.

Tom swung his legs up on the bed and scooted closer to her. "Eleanora, talk to me!"

"You want to talk? Okay. Let's talk." Her voice was furious—more angry than he'd ever heard it. It lashed his ears like an ice-cold wind. "I saw her. I saw that woman with you at the library this morning. I gather she's someone you've known for a while. I know you're supposed to see her tomorrow. I know that we only got married out of convenience and you're staying with me out of some misguided sense of honor, but you don't have to do that, Tom! You can go and . . . go and . . ." Her voice broke as it was enveloped in sobs, and her shoulders shook from the force of her weeping.

Without asking her permission, he whipped the covers down, picked her up in his arms and deposited her on his lap, wrapping his arms around her and holding her as hard as he could without crushing her. He dropped his lips to her sweet-smelling hair over and over again, kissing her as she sobbed, as she let go of all the ugliness she'd been holding on to all day.

Apparently, she'd seen him talking to Charity this morning.

And gotten the wrong idea.

"I do want to talk," he said gently, rubbing her back. "When you're ready to listen."

"I . . . I know I'm y-young and I'm not very c-cultured. B-but I would've tried my b-best to make you h-h-happy, Tom."

"You *do* make me happy, sunshine."

"Then why . . . ?" she sobbed, dropping her forehead on his shoulder but trying to push him away at the same time.

He held on tightly to her. "Whenever you're ready to listen . . ." he said again.

She took a jagged, sobby breath and stopped fighting him, letting her body go slack against his. And he held her, resting his lips against her hair as his hands made lazy strokes up and down her back.

"F-fine," she said. "Talk."

"You saw me talking to Charity Gordon, who is Dean Gordon's daughter and whom I've known since I was a student at Kinsey."

She took a deep, ragged breath and sighed. "S-skinny-dipping?"

He forced himself not to laugh. "Her, not me. *She* was skinny-dipping with a couple of guys from our class. Van and I stole their clothes. End of story."

"So she . . . she never saw you naked?"

"Nope," said Tom, gentling his hold on her.

She squared her shoulders.

"Why are you seeing her *tomorrow*?" she asked, her voice accusatory.

"Because you and I were invited for dinner at the dean's house on New Year's Day, and I forgot to mention it to you. I see your face every evening, and I get so distracted. It slipped my mind."

She leaned back and looked at him, searching his face with puffy, red, watery eyes. "D-dinner? With the d-dean?"

Suddenly, she launched herself back into his arms, shuddering with the force of her tears, and Tom was so confused, he was almost alarmed.

"Baby? Why are you crying? There's nothing between me and Charity. Eleanora, I swear to you, there never *was*, but there definitely isn't now. I'm in love with *you*. I'm in love with my wife. I can't even imagine wanting to be with another woman. Sunshine, you have to believe me. You're everything to me."

"And you're everything to me," she mumbled against his shirt, which was wet from her tears. "I love you so much, Tom."

"Then please tell me why you're still upset. There's nothing going on between me and Charity. You and I love each other. It's okay, right?"

She shook her head and said "No" in a very small voice.

"Look at me, baby." She leaned back, and he tipped her chin up. "Why isn't it okay?"

"Because I lied to you. There's nothing wrong with the car," she said, looking guilty and sniffling at the same time.

"You made me walk home because you were mad?"

She nodded.

He took a beat to think this over. It kind of sucked that she hadn't given him the benefit of the doubt, but the reality was that they'd hadn't known each other that long. Trust was something that still needed to be built between them.

"Try to trust me next time?"

She nodded.

"Good, because it was a cold walk."

"I'm sorry," she said.

"We okay now?"

"Mm-hm," she said.

"Smile for me," he said, leaning forward to brush her lips with his. "There's no one for me but you. Don't you know that?"

"I do now," she said.

He slipped off the bed, taking off his jacket and hanging it up before looking back down at her. "So, what's for dinner? I saw it on the table downstairs. I was thinking you might have made your breakfast casserole special since it's New Year's Eve."

She winced, pulling her bottom lip into her mouth.

"Oh no," she groaned.

"What?"

"Remember this morning? The, uh, the Paul Newman quote? The one you told me?" she asked, looking downright sheepish before dropping his eyes.

He nodded, sitting down on the bed beside her, not sure where she was going.

"Yeah."

"Dinner is . . . hamburger," she said softly, staring down at her lap. Then, lifting her chin, she met his eyes and added, "A big plate of raw hamburger."

Chapter 14

Tom stared at her in shock for several long seconds before his lips tilted up, slowly at first, then wider and wider, until she realized he was laughing.

"Sunshine, even when you're pissed as hell, you're still spectacular."

He reached for her then, pulling her on top of him, and she covered his face with kisses, her relief as palpable as her love was strong, and in between smooches, she promised that she'd never get jealous again, though she was fairly certain they both knew that was a big, fat lie.

Tom flipped her over and deepened their kisses until they were strung out on passion. Trailing his lips along the column of her neck, he whispered that he loved her, that she had no reason, ever, to be jealous. He pulled off her sweatshirt, and his lips skimmed through the valley of her bare breasts, scalding her tummy, then pushing down her underwear to kiss the secret, hidden parts of her body. He worshipped her with his lips and tongue until she screamed his name and climaxed in boneless waves of awesome. And only then did he unbuckle his belt, pull down his pants, and slip inside her, groaning that she made him happy as she slid her ankles up his legs and locked them around his waist.

After making love, they faced each other in bed, Tom's hand resting on her hip as he told her shocking stories about Charity Gordon, stories that made her gasp and giggle, proclaiming Eve Marie the far less slutty of the two.

Later, she cut up some onions and potatoes and fried them with the hamburger, which meant that instead of the fine meal she'd envisioned, they dined on hamburger hash and two leftover beers for their first New Year's Eve as man and wife. Good intentions notwithstanding, it was the best hamburger hash she'd ever had in her entire life.

As they drove to the Gordons' house the next evening, Eleanora reflected on the wonder of the previous night— how she'd felt so frightened and heartbroken before she learned the truth about Tom's disinterest in Charity, and how his voice and assurances and strong arms around her body could whisk away all the fear and potential heartbreak like it never even existed.

She smoothed her hands on her black, ankle-length skirt—the same one she'd worn the day she met Tom's grandfather—and hoped that her simple, white angora sweater didn't look too cheap. She liked how soft and feminine it felt against her skin, and from the way Tom had looked at her when she met him downstairs, she knew he approved.

As they pulled into Dean Gordon's driveway, Tom turned to her.

"I doubt Charity will be inappropriate since we're here together, but please, baby, just trust me that I have zero interest in her. Never did, never will."

She cleared her throat and smiled at Tom, then leaned over the bolster and kissed him. "Don't worry about it, Tom. It's going to be fine."

Because if Charity Gordon does decide to be inappropriate, it won't go well for her, thought Eleanora.

Tom was *her* husband, and if she needed to proverbially piss on his leg a little in front of the flirtatious Miss Gordon to be certain that territory borders would be respected in the future, so be it. She'd stay well hydrated, just in case.

Tom kept his hand on the small of her back as they stepped up the walkway to the Gordons' house, and Eleanora reached out to ring the doorbell, taking a deep breath in an effort to quiet her nerves. Her last foray into Tom's world had been the furthest possible thing from pleasant, with the elder Mr. English calling her a slut and worse. She braced herself for unpleasantness, and—surprise! surprise!—immediately found it in the form of Charity Gordon.

"Tom!" she exclaimed, opening the door and offering Tom a beaming smile. Her eyes flicked momentarily to Eleanora, but didn't rest long. "I'm delighted you're here! Come in!"

Tom stayed rooted where he stood, his hand still flush on Eleanora's back, and said, "I'd like to introduce to you my wife, Eleanora."

"Hmm," said Charity, sliding her eyes to Eleanora with all the warmth of a python. "Yes. Welcome."

"Thank you," said Eleanora evenly, stepping inside.

Tom helped her with her coat, then handed them both to Charity. She draped them over her arm and gestured to the hallway off the foyer.

"Tom, my father's in the living room. My brother, Alex, is visiting, and Geoffrey's come up for the holiday. Go say hello."

Tom looked at Eleanora, asking her with his eyes if she was okay. She grinned at him and winked, and he kissed her cheek before heading off to find the other men.

"So," said Eleanora, watching as Charity hung their coats on hangers and closed the closet door. "Thanks for having us."

Charity turned around, giving Eleanora a frosty smile. "What was your name again?"

"Mrs. English," she responded.

Eyes narrowed, Charity clarified, "Your *first* name."

"Eleanora."

Clearly she'd thought that Eleanora would be some coltish pushover. Well, she wasn't. She'd lived through far worse than Charity Gordon could imagine.

"Eleanora English. Well, that's ridiculously alliterative."

"I prefer to think of it as melodic."

"I'm sure you do," said Charity, eyeing Eleanora with interest.

Eleanora endured her perusal without flinching.

"You're not what I expected," Charity finally said. Her eyes flicked down Eleanora's sweater and skirt, sizing up the younger woman. "And you're very young."

"I probably seem that way to *you*," said Eleanora, referring to their decade age difference. "But I'm certainly old enough to be married."

She wouldn't be pushed around, and she wouldn't let another woman make a move on what was hers. And Tom belonged to her.

Charity's smile, which had been frosty in the first place, disappeared, leaving a thin line of red-painted lips behind.

"Recent reports mark a higher chance of divorce for young, impetuous couples." Charity tapped her chin. "Daddy says you married very quickly."

"Yes, we did," she said. "And, you know, I recently read a report that said your chances of surviving marriage—or *an engagement*, for that matter—are better if you're not a total bitch."

Charity's eyes narrowed as she gasped.

"I may as well add that your unspoken suspicions are entirely true: Tom's dynamite in bed. However, that said, he's mine, Charity, so I'll thank you not to visit him at the library anymore and embarrass yourself by inviting him out on private lunch dates." Eleanora smiled congenially, but her eyes felt fierce, focused on Charity's like lasers. "All clear?"

Charity sputtered, "I . . . well, I . . ."

"Shall we join the others?"

Eleanora spun around and walked in the general direction that Tom had headed, her heart thumping uncomfortably even as she made an effort to look as cool as a cucumber. Thankfully, it didn't take long to find him, in front of a crackling fire, surrounded by three other men who looked equally rich and preppy. She sighed, then waved at him from the doorway of the room, and he excused himself to come to her.

His eyes scanned her face. "Everything okay?"

"The proverbial leg pissing is done."

"What?"

"Don't worry. I won. Introduce me?"

He leaned down and pressed his warm lips to her cheek. "Tell me all about it later."

"You bet," she said, letting him lead her over to the other men.

"Gentlemen," said Tom, "may I present my wife, Eleanora English?"

To Eleanora's left was the eldest of the three men, whom she assumed to be Dean Gordon.

"My dear," he said warmly, taking her hand, "what a delight. You are very welcome."

"Thank you," she answered, with a genuine smile of her own, wondering how a shrew like Charity had such a congenial father. "Tom is so looking forward to working with you."

"And I him." Dean Gordon looked at the young man to his left. "You must meet my son, Alex."

Eleanora held out her hand, and Alex grabbed it eagerly, his eyes dipping to her breasts for a moment before returning to her face. "A pleasure, ahem, Mrs. English."

"For me too," she said, smiling at the young man.

He grinned back at her, his smile impish. *Oh, you're trouble*, she thought, pulling her hand away from his tight grasp with a little tug.

"And this," said Tom, "is Geoffrey Atwell. Geoff and I were at Kinsey together."

Eleanora turned away from flirty Alex and met eyes with a man who looked considerably older than Tom, despite the fact that they were the same age. His blond hair was thinning, and his blue eyes looked tired. She remembered Tom mentioning to her that Geoffrey was Charity's erstwhile fiancé, and her heart went out to him.

"Hello, Geoffrey," she said warmly.

"Happy New Year," he answered with a grim smile, taking a long sip of his drink.

"I hope it will be," she said.

"Of course it will be," said Charity, entering the room and taking Geoffrey's arm with a big show.

He brightened suddenly, his face losing years as he looked down hopefully at his ex-fiancée's hand on his arm.

Poor man, thought Eleanora. *It's obvious he's crazy for her and*—from what Tom had told her—*Charity's just stringing him along.*

Charity's eyes swept over Eleanora and slid to Tom, where they lingered for a moment, her lips turning down when she didn't find what she was looking for. Eleanora felt Tom's arm slip around her waist and his lips press tenderly to her temple. She was waiting when Charity met her eyes with a flinty expression.

You see, said the look she gave Charity. *He's mine.*

"Dinner's ready," said Charity, turning to her sad-sack ex-fiancé. "Come, Geoffrey. I've switched things around and put you next to me, after all."

Charity's ridiculous rivalry with Eleanora strained things at the table for the first course, but by the second, Dean Gordon had taken over the conversation with a discussion of future improvements at Kinsey, and with four graduates at the table, they didn't lack for opinions or debate.

One thing that bothered Tom, aside from Charity's frosty treatment of his wife, was the way she was treating Geoffrey. If he'd been better friends with Geoffrey, Tom would have pulled him aside and told him to run for the hills—reminding him that there were a million delightful girls in Boston, where Geoffrey was from, or in New York, where he lived and worked—and advised him to find some sweet girl who could make him happy. But Geoffrey only seemed to have eyes for Charity, delighted when she gave him a moment of attention, and subdued but accepting when she made eyes at Tom.

It made him extra grateful for what he'd somehow managed to find with Eleanora—someone who had quickly become his whole world, but who loved him back in equal measure. How terrible to be in a relationship with someone when it was clear you were the one who loved harder and better, and always would. What a lonely way to live, to know that the love you bore would never be returned, that your heart would ache for more, and more would never be forthcoming.

And suddenly he was reminded of a verse from one of Elizabeth Barrett Browning's sonnets: "*The face of all the world is changed, I think, / Since first I heard the footsteps of thy soul.*"

Under the table, he reached for his wife's hand and squeezed it with unending gratitude. For finding her. For her love. For the right to love her. For the footsteps of her soul across the landscape of his heart.

After dessert, she turned to him. "The bathroom?"

"I'm guessing it's in the front hallway," he whispered, standing as she excused herself, and noticing when Alex Gordon left the table not a moment later.

He would have had to be blind not to notice the way Alex had been staring at Eleanora from across the table, and after a few minutes of polite conversation, on which Tom could barely focus, he excused himself as well, hopeful that he'd intercept his wife before Alex did.

He stopped just short of the vestibule, standing in a dark hallway between the dining room and front foyer, as he heard Alex Gordon's voice ask, "Can I ask you a question?"

"Okay," said Eleanora.

"How old are you? Twenty-one? Twenty-two?"

"Around there."

Alex's cocky voice continued. "Then why on earth are you with an old man like Tom English? For God's sake, he could be your father."

"Sure. If he fathered me at nine," she said dryly.

"Come on, sweets. You know what I mean. He's old. He's dull. You're too young and too foxy to be tied down. I mean, your ass? It's a thing of total beauty, and I say that having attended college in New York City for the past three years. I've known many beautiful women and never had any complaints. Let's get out of here and go have some real fun. What do you say?"

She chuckled as though his words were genuinely amusing, and Tom pressed his hand to his chest, sucking in a painful breath and holding it.

Alex Gordon was right. She was young and beautiful, and Tom was quickly heading into his midthirties. Right now, he was different from other men she'd met, and maybe that made him seem unique or special to her. But sooner than later, she'd be able to move fluidly in his world of privilege. How long until she realized that she could have any man in his social set? Any of his peers, including the younger ones? The richer ones? How long until she realized she'd made a bad deal and wanted out? Wanted someone younger and cooler?

He quieted his mind as she spoke again. "It's Alex, right?"

"It is," he said, his voice low and suggestive.

"I like the name Alex."

"There's a lot more to like than my name, kitten. I promise you that."

"Alex, do you know how Tom and I met?"

"Sure. In Vail."

"On the slopes?" she asked.

"I'm assuming. Or through friends."

"Through friends," she repeated, laughing softly. "How about my education? What do you figure?"

"Bryn Mawr? Vassar?"

She sighed. "Are either of those near Princeton?"

He chuckled as though she'd made an amusing remark. "So you went to Princeton."

"No, Alex. I didn't go to Princeton."

There was a pause, and Tom's lips twitched as he remembered the first time he'd ever seen his wife, giving a forward skier hell when he'd had the indecency to proposition her at Auntie Rose's. By the tone of her voice, he was fairly certain he knew what was coming next, and he exhaled softly, relaxing against the wall behind him to enjoy it.

"Alex, when Tom and I met, almost two weeks ago, I was a waitress in a twenty-four-hour diner in Vail. I *guess* you could say we met through friends. My cousin was trying to, well—let's just be honest here—*bang* Tom's friend Van. She was a waitress too."

"Fine," he said tersely. "Have a laugh at my expense."

"I'm not having a laugh. I'm from Romero, Colorado. You've never heard of it. The extent of my education is some night classes at Colorado Mountain College. You've never heard of *it* either. We have no mutual friends. And I certainly didn't go to Princeton."

"Well," said Alex, and Tom imagined him fumbling now because there was no way to mistake the sincerity in Eleanora's voice. "I just . . . I assumed . . ."

"Alex? Can I give you some advice?"

"Well, I . . . I guess so."

"Don't assume. It makes an ass out of you and me," she said, and Tom had to bite his lip to squelch a guffaw of laughter. *Poor Alex Gordon.* "The reason I married Tom English, the reason I fell in love with him, and the reason I will stay faithfully married to him until the day I die, despite our age difference and our wildly dissimilar backgrounds, is this: Tom saw beyond a waitress uniform. Tom didn't give a—forgive me—*shit* about my lack of connections, and my crappy, incomplete education was never a blip on his radar. He treated me with respect from the start. And though I'm sure he *noticed* my ass, he *touched* my heart. And he was the first man . . ." She laughed softly, and Tom wondered what was coming next. ". . . who didn't treat me like meat."

He got the joke and laughed silently to himself.

"In short, Alex," she finished, "he wasn't a jerk."

"I never said he was," Alex rallied back defensively. "Tom's a fine—"

She continued as if he hadn't spoken. "Don't be a jerk, Alex. You're what? Twenty? Twenty-one?"

"Twenty-one," he confirmed, his voice strained. "Almost."

"Almost twenty-one," she repeated gently, and Tom imagined her smiling at Alex Gordon, showing him a little mercy. "You still have time to learn how to *stop* being a jerk before it's too late. Don't squander it, huh?"

"I think I'll go back in and join the others," said Alex, his voice low and embarrassed.

"That's fine. But to answer your question? I say no, Alex. Thank you for asking, but I'm happily married to my husband, so no, I'm not interested in leaving him here and going off with you."

Tom heard her heels move on the hardwood floor, and she rounded the corner, standing before him in the dim hallway, her eyes widening in surprise to find him suddenly in front of her.

"Tom," she whispered.

"You're fucking amazing," he murmured, grabbing her arm and pulling her against his chest.

She grinned at him. "You heard all of that?"

"Every word."

"And?"

"I'd take you up against this wall if we were alone," he said, his lips landing on the hot skin of her throat. He skimmed them to her ear, biting the lobe, his cock hardening as she gasped.

"Let's go," she said, her voice a cross between a whimper and a sigh. "I don't care if it's rude. I want to go home. I want you."

Pulling her against his side, he escorted her back down the hallway to the dining room. "Neville, thanks so much for your hospitality tonight, but my wife has a bit of a headache. I think we should head home."

"Yes, of course," said Neville, standing up and offering his hand first to Tom, then to Eleanora. "Can I get you some aspirin for the ride home, my dear?"

"No, thank you. Nothing that a few hours in bed won't fix," she said, darting a quick glance to Charity before smiling warmly at her father. "Thank you for having us. Dinner was delicious, and the company was . . . interesting."

They said the rest of their good-byes quickly, and Tom retrieved their coats on the way out the door, holding her hand as they walked down the icy path to his car. But Alex Gordon's words circled in his head: *He's old. He's dull. You're too young and too foxy to be tied down.* He needed to be sure that her response to Alex wasn't just loyalty and bravado.

"I *am* older than you," he said, starting the engine.

"Yep."

"And though I don't like to think of myself as dull, I did drag you out to the middle of nowhere, Connecticut, to embark on an exciting career of teaching English."

"Tom."

"Yes?"

"Shut up," she said, giving him an annoyed look before turning back to the windshield.

"I think we should talk about it," he pushed. "I think—"

"I mean it, Tom. Shut up until we get home, or I might hit you and make you swerve off the road, killing us both, which would be a really bad start to the new year."

Grumbling softly, he drove home the rest of the way in silence, pulling into the driveway in front of their house and cutting the engine. He looked over at her in the dim light provided by the moon and stars, but her expression was set in stone as she stared out the windshield.

Exiting the car, he rounded it and opened her door, helping her out.

As she stood up before him, she drew her palm back and let it crack across his cheek.

"What the . . . what the *hell*?"

"Do I have your attention?"

He winced. "Fuck. Yes. That hurt."

"Good. And if I allude to the New Year's I smacked your face, do you think you'll remember it fifty years from now?"

He rubbed his cheek, which burned despite the subzero temperature. "Uh, yeah, I think so."

"Great," she said, slipping her hand under his to cup his cheek with her bare palm, caressing it gently. "Then listen to me, husband." Her face was bright and serious as she searched his eyes, seeking collusion. Her other palm landed on his other cheek, and she cradled his face, forcing his gaze. "I don't care how long I've known you. I know your heart as well as my own. I don't care how much older you are than me. It's just a number and completely irrelevant. And I cannot imagine a day when I think you're dull. Aside from the fact that I want to be in your bed every minute . . ." She stepped closer, and Tom opened his cashmere coat, wrapping it around both of them and holding her tight. ". . . I think you're fucking brilliant and fascinating, and I will never, ever get tired of you." His heart pumped like crazy, his ears drinking in the paradise of her words. "I love you. And fifty years from now, if you ask me these questions again, I will give you the same answers I gave you on the night I smacked your face. Because I will feel exactly the same. Got it?"

He gripped her so tightly, it was a wonder she could draw breath, but she did. Her chest swelled with air, her breasts pushing into his chest as she rested her cheek on his shoulder.

"I'm an idiot," he sighed, resting his cheek on her hair.

"You're a newlywed," she countered gently.

"So are you."

"And the raw hamburger fiasco is still very fresh," she reminded him. "We're finding our way, but I just . . . I have this feeling, and it's so strong, Tom. *So strong*." She took a big, deep breath and sighed with contentment. "We're going to make it. I know it. We're going to be okay."

Tom kissed the top of her head and looked up at the sky. He couldn't ever remember a sky so clear—there were so many millions of stars, they almost blended, twinkling and resplendent, into a bright and hopeful eternity.

"I want to make love to you," he murmured close to her ear. "I want you whimpering beneath me. I want you crying out my name. I want to be . . . one."

She tipped her head back, looking up at him with dark, wide eyes. Then, without a word, she took his hand and led him into their little house, where she answered his every want with her own, and promised her love was his until the end of time.

Chapter 15

Weeks passed quickly once the boys returned to Kinsey, and Eleanora, who simply wasn't cut out to be a lady of leisure, convinced Tom how much happier she'd be with a part-time job. She found one at the village pharmacy in Cornwall, working as a clerk and cashier five days a week. She arrived at work at seven thirty after dropping off Tom at Kinsey, and left at two o'clock, two hours before she had to fetch him from school, which left time for keeping their house and running errands.

This morning, the first Friday of February, was one of those especially beautiful winter mornings when one could be tricked, just for a day, into thinking that spring is imminent. Despite the seven or eight inches of snow on the ground, the sun was shining and high when Eleanora woke up, and the weather forecast called for a high of fifty-seven degrees. She left her coat at home and opted for a turtleneck and sweater, delighting in the unseasonably warm day.

Tom kissed her passionately in the parking lot at Kinsey, and she accused him of having spring fever.

"You know the boys have their noses pressed up against the windows watching us," she said, feeling dizzy and breathless as she grinned at him.

"Where else are they going to learn how to kiss a woman?"

"Ah, I see. You're giving them a lesson?"

"On loving? No, baby. That's the lesson you're giving me."

"What's gotten into you? Spring fever?"

"It *does* feel like spring today," he said, threading his fingers through her hair and pulling her closer. "Kiss me again."

His lips touched down on hers, demanding and hungry, and she closed her eyes, letting herself be swept away by the strong pressure of his lips, his hand in her hair, his other hand holding her jaw. He stole her thoughts and her breath, leaving her befuddled and gasping when he finally pulled away with a satisfied grin.

"No flirting at the pharmacy," he said, winking at her.

"With whom? Old Mr. Jenkins? Not even."

"I love you tons," he said, picking up his briefcase from the floor.

"I love you back," she answered, waving at him as he left her.

And then *it* happened again.

Again, because it had been happening a lot lately, this sudden feeling that the world was spinning. It was almost how Eleanora felt when she'd had too much to drink and lay down on her bed. The world would spin and spin, leaving her slightly nauseous and a little worried. She closed her eyes and clutched the steering wheel, and after a moment, just like the other times, it passed. She shook her head and sighed. Tom *had* just kissed the life out of her.

Grinning at her reflection in the rearview mirror, she backed out of the Kinsey faculty parking lot and headed to the Cornwall Pharmacy.

As she got out of the car, her purse strap broke, and her bag landed in the muddy snow of the parking lot. Bending over to pick it up, she heard the unmistakable *rrrrrrip* sound of her pants splitting down the backside.

"Oh, come on!" she exclaimed, standing up quickly to be sure no one saw her underwear. She twisted to try to see the damage, but couldn't. Cradling her broken purse in her arms, she closed the car door and trudged into work.

Once inside, she put the contents of her purse in a shopping bag and took off her cardigan sweater, tying it around her waist. That would just have to do until she could change later, and clearly she needed to lay off the recipe books filled with rich foods. Lately, she'd been trying out all sorts of not-breakfast-for-dinner recipes on Tom, and though she wouldn't say she had a knack for making the dishes *look* good, they certainly *tasted* terrific.

"Morning, Ellie!" yelled Mr. Jenkins, waving at her from the pharmacy, located just behind and above the cashier area.

"My name's Eleanora," she said under her breath, smiling cheerfully and waving back. He couldn't hear her from behind the high plexiglass wall that separated the store from the prescription drugs. He'd been calling her Ellie since the day she'd accepted the job, and she didn't have the heart to correct him anymore. His ears turned bright red whenever she did, so she could tell he didn't mean to keep making the mistake.

"Morning, Eleanora," said Kristin, Eleanora's coworker and Mr. Jenkins's youngest daughter.

"Hey, hot stuff," she said, smiling at the sweet-natured redhead. She reminded Eleanora a lot of Evie, and since Kristin was her only real friend in the area, she meant a lot to Eleanora.

"One of us is *hot stuff*," said Kristin, dropping her eyes to Eleanora's breasts, which strained against her simple, light-blue turtleneck shirt, "but it ain't me!"

Eleanora looked down at her chest, noticing how her breasts spilled a little over the cups of her bra, creating two crests of extra boob. She groaned. Further evidence that she needed to lay off the rich dinners.

"I think I need to go on a diet."

"Bet Tom doesn't mind," said Kristin, winking at her friend. "Hey, Dad asked us to restock the feminine hygiene supplies. You want to do it? Or should I?"

"I don't mind," said Eleanora, grabbing the big box of tampons and pads from the counter. "You can work the register."

"Want to have lunch later? We could swing over to the deli and grab sandwiches?"

Eleanora grinned and nodded. "Sure. Sounds good. But stop me if I order anything but Tab and salad."

She headed over to aisle four and knelt on the floor with a price gun, her easy exchange with Kristin making her mind segue to Evie's latest letter from Hong Kong. Evie had definitely made the right choice for her life. She liked working for Mr. and Mrs. Holmes and had definitely fallen in love with the children she was minding. She'd also fallen in love with Hong Kong, which she described with childish delight in every letter—the food, the language, the people, so different from those at home.

Evie had also fallen head over heels in love with Van. Not that Eleanora was surprised, but part of her wished she'd been there to see the process of Van and Evie truly falling for each other. And in such a romantic place too. Evie gushed about the harbor lights at night, the clubs where Van took her dancing, and the posh hotel suite where she stayed with him one night a week. She reassured Eleanora that he was taking good care of her, and Eleanora believed her, laughing and crying as she read each letter. She laughed because she was happy for Evie and cried because she missed her cousin so terribly.

For someone who'd had relatively little family in her life, Eleanora longed for family in an increasingly painful way. She wished that Evie and Van could meet her and Tom for dinner on the weekends, or that when she had big news, she could run to Evie's house and burst into her kitchen to share it. She grieved that she was so alone in the world and that Tom, in standing up for their marriage, was now as alone as she. Where would they go for holidays? What would they tell their children when they asked about aunts, uncles, and grandparents?

Tears welled up in Eleanora's eyes, and she looked down at the tampon box in her hand, running the price gun over the box and placing it listlessly on the shelf. Her eyes lingered on the box, widening as a thought came together in her head at an alarming speed, bearing an extremely alarming meaning.

Ripping the tampon box back off the shelf, her heart rate tripled as she held it in her trembling hands.

She hadn't bought tampons since December. Since before she had met Tom. Because—*oh my God! How did I miss this?*—she hadn't had a period since then.

Letting the box drop from her shaking fingers, she counted back. She'd had her period in December, right? Right. She and Evie had been on the same cycle, and she remembered Evie commenting happily that they wouldn't have their periods on New Year's Eve . . . which meant she'd gotten it just before meeting Tom. And she'd met Tom, let's see, one, two, four, six, *ohmygod*, almost nine weeks ago.

Nine weeks without a period.

She didn't notice that her hands had somehow drifted to her belly, covering it protectively as she put other details together in her head—her occasional dizzy spells, her expanded waistline, her overflowing breasts.

"But we were careful," she whispered. "He always pulled out. *Always.*"

Except, Eleanora was a bright girl, and she knew—as well as anyone else—that even if you were supercareful about pulling out, there was always that small chance that a swimmer or two could get away.

Her eyes welled with tears as she flicked her glance to the nearby pregnancy tests, stood up, and plucked one from the shelf. She hid it under her sweater and beelined for the bathroom, avoiding Kristin.

After she'd peed in a cup, dripped three drops of urine into a test tube, added a chemical included in the test, and shaken it up, she set it back in the test holder and hid it under the sink, in the back corner, behind the extra toilet tissue. In two hours she'd know for sure.

But as she walked back into the store, headed for aisle four, her heart already knew. She was pregnant with Tom's baby—with their first child—and though she was frightened on one hand, her heart swelled with the sort of love she'd reserved heretofore for Tom. A baby that was half him and half her, and all theirs. It was so marvelous, so amazing and miraculous, she gulped over the growing lump in her throat, biting her lip to keep from giggling or crying.

A little Elizabeth, she thought, kneeling back down on the floor. *Or a little Barrett.*

She'd never met anyone named Barrett, but it sounded very grand, and it seemed only right that their child should be named after Elizabeth Barrett Browning. After all, their mutual love for her poetry had lit the fire of passion between them from the very beginning.

She sat back on the pharmacy carpet, placing her hands tentatively on her still-flat abdomen, and summoned Tom's favorite words by Browning, which he shared with her frequently: *You were made perfectly to be loved—and surely I have loved you, in the idea of you, my whole life long.*

Yes, thought Eleanora, gently rubbing her tummy. *I have loved you, in the idea of you, my whole life long, little baby.*

She felt a bewildering, joyful burst of happiness bubble up inside her, spreading from the very depths of her heart to the tips of her fingers and everywhere in between.

She and Tom were going to have a baby.

On his lunch break, Tom opened his checkbook, as if waiting a few hours before looking at it again would somehow make a thousand dollars magically appear.

It didn't.

The balance read exactly as it had earlier in the day, after he'd paid their rent and January bills: $708.27. That's what they had. That's *all* they had.

Tom, who had never lived in the real world, had thought that five thousand dollars would last for months. But he hadn't counted on deposits for the phone, water, and electric service. He hadn't anticipated that even the cheapest furnishings would cost over a thousand dollars, with extra for delivery. How could he have known that when Eleanora complained of sinus pressure and he told her to see a doctor, that it would end up costing over two hundred dollars for the visit and her prescription antibiotics? Not to mention the cost of clothes and groceries, shampoo and deodorant, snow shovels and garbage bags and someone to tote the garbage away. It all cost something. And it added up so quickly, it made Tom's head spin.

The reality was this: living on one thousand dollars a month was *only* possible if there were no unforeseen expenses, no unpleasant little surprises. One doctor's visit or transmission problem or long-distance phone call could bury the month.

He took a deep breath and sighed, closing the little bankbook and shoving it back inside his desk. It worried him that they had no savings, no recourse should an unexpected expense suddenly appear. And living in Weston didn't exactly afford Tom lucrative opportunities to make more money. It had hurt his pride a little when Eleanora decided to go back to work. Not that he didn't respect women in the workforce—he did. But the women of his social class didn't work much anyway, and they certainly didn't work once they were married. It shamed him that he and Eleanora found themselves in a circumstance wherein her small income was actually helpful.

Taking his lunch out of the bottom drawer of his desk, he looked at the outside of the brown paper bag and, despite his worries, couldn't help but grin. She'd drawn a smiley face with the words "I love you silly" written underneath. Inside, Tom found his regular lunch: a ham sandwich, a thermos of chicken noodle soup, and an apple. Though Kinsey subsidized lunch for the faculty, he'd still have had to pay forty dollars a month, which simply wasn't worth it.

He unscrewed the top of the thermos and took a spoon from his top drawer, looking out at the asphalt basketball court as his soup cooled a little. Generally, the boys huddled in bunches, trying to stay warm for the thirty minutes they spent outside. But today they were enjoying the brief burst of sunshine and warmth. Some played basketball on the slushy blacktop while others seemed to be playing tag. He wished he could share their lightheartedness, but his thoughts wandered back to his bankbook, and he huffed softly. What was the answer?

He took a sip of soup, thinking of the unopened letter from his grandfather in his coat pocket. Quite sure of what it contained, Tom hadn't seen any point in opening it. Anything that insulted or threatened his marriage was unacceptable and unwelcome in his life. Giving up Eleanora was unthinkable, and he wouldn't beg for his grandfather to give her a chance either. Peace at that cost would mean that Eleanora would never be treated like an English. If he crawled back to Haverford Park on his knees, she'd always be seen as the albatross that had led him to beg for his birthright. No, if he and Eleanora ever returned to Haverford Park, it would be after his grandfather apologized and issued a respectful invitation. Anything less couldn't be considered.

Tom had watched his father, Bertram, get beaten down by his grandfather's threats and iron-fisted control. Once affable and easygoing, as Neville Gordon had indicated, Bertram English was now a spiritless, tired, empty shirt. The sum of his life added up to a handful of broken relationships: two sons who barely knew each other, an alcoholic ex-wife he'd loved deeply, a current wife he didn't seem to love very much at all, a father who had never really respected him, a job he likely despised but tolerated because it was expected of him . . .

. . . and a very flush bank account.

Tom supposed that, in his father's eyes, the flush bank account made the rest of it worthwhile. Or had, at one point in time.

Before her dreams were thrust aside, Tom's mother, Rebecca, had been one of the more promising violinists in New York City, and his father had been one of the more promising cellists. But music wasn't at all a suitable profession for an English, and Bertram had been brought to heel with mounting pressure to do his duty and threats of being cut off.

Unlike Tom, Bertram had caved. He'd gone to work for English & Son, dragging his unhappy wife and small son to live at Haverford Park. Tom's father had clipped his mother's wings and gotten a life of riches in return. Meanwhile, Rebecca English had been betrayed. Listless and depressed, consigned to the life of society matron when she'd hoped to be a concert violinist, she'd never quite recovered from Bertram's betrayal. She'd turned to drink, and little by little, she wasn't a wife or a mother anymore at all; she was the mistress to whatever brand of gin was her favorite. As her violin gathered dust in the top of her closet, Tom was neglected before being shipped off to Kinsey, and Bertram was eventually pressured to divorce his drunken embarrassment of a wife.

Thus had Tom's family been shattered.

And he would not, under any circumstances, let history repeat itself.

Unless Eleanora's talents and aspirations were as respected and supported as his own, Tom was adamant that they would not return to Philadelphia, nor take a dime of English money. He wouldn't knuckle under to his grandfather for access to his trust. He wouldn't dishonor his wife by making amends with the man who'd insulted her. Eleanora would come first. And *only* Eleanora.

He finished the soup and screwed the thermos lid back on, then started on the sandwich.

His lofty sense of honor, however, wouldn't pay the rent. Tom needed to make more money.

A knock at his classroom door made him look up, then beckon Neville Gordon to come in.

"Mind if I join you, Tom?"

"Not at all," said Tom, gesturing to his desk, which had plenty of room for Dean Gordon to sit across from him.

Neville pulled a chair from one of the student's desks and sat down. "Please eat. I don't mean to interrupt your lunch."

Tom took a bite of his sandwich, chewing as Neville cleared his throat.

"I've had to let Milton Smiley go."

Milton Smiley was the young phys ed teacher who'd also acted as the faculty resident adviser for one of four Kinsey dormitories.

"Huh," exclaimed Tom, placing his sandwich down on the waxed paper it had been wrapped in. "Sorry to hear that."

"He had a girl in his room last Friday night. Three of the boys saw her. More than that, *heard* her," said Neville, shaking his head disdainfully. "Can you imagine what the parents will say when they find out? At least by firing Milton, we've headed it off."

"He was young," said Tom, picturing the twenty-something teacher in his head. He wasn't much older than Eleanora.

Neville sighed. "It's left me in a pickle, though."

"How's that?"

"Don't have anyone to be resident adviser at Cambridge Hall for now." Neville lifted his head as he said this, meeting Tom's eyes meaningfully. "Could use a solid, married man to take over for a while."

Tom concealed a wince.

"How much does it pay?"

"One hundred dollars a week."

Tom gulped, nodding, feeling miserable. Four hundred dollars more a month would increase his salary by almost fifty percent.

"Hours?"

"Monday through Saturday. Six o'clock p.m. until eight o'clock a.m."

"And Sundays?" asked Tom softly.

"Seniors man the dorms one night a week for leadership credits."

"I see."

Neville took a deep breath and sighed. "I wouldn't have mentioned it except when you took the job, well, you asked about ancillary income, so—"

"Yes," said Tom. "Yes, I did."

"It's only until May," said Neville. "Maybe not even that long if we can find and hire a new phys ed teacher before. I've already sent out some feelers."

Four months. Four months of not sleeping next to his wife. Four months of wishing he was beside her as he slept across town in a dorm that smelled of gym socks and lead pencils.

His father had chosen money over love, and look where that had gotten him.

But Tom knew it wasn't fair to compare the two circumstances. It was one thing not to *take* his grandfather's money, but quite another not to *make* the money he needed to support Eleanora when it was offered to him.

"Give me until tomorrow to decide?" he asked, hating the words as they passed through his lips.

"Take until Monday," said Neville, giving him a sorry look as he pushed up from his seat and exited the classroom quietly.

Tom wrapped up the last of his sandwich, his appetite gone. When he looked out the window, the playground was empty, and the bright sunshine was gone. Storm clouds were rolling in, over the landscape, over Tom's heart.

Chapter 16

The test hidden in the back of the bathroom cabinet at work only confirmed what Eleanora already knew to be true: she was expecting, and, if her calculations were right, she'd be a mother sometime in September. With her precious news pressed close to her heart, she spent the rest of the afternoon imagining the best way to tell Tom that he was going to be become a father. Taking fifty dollars from her dwindling savings, she went to the IGA and bought two filets mignons, baking potatoes, and fresh-baked croissants. In the bakery section, she purchased two vanilla cupcakes, one with "It's a girl!" written in pink, and another with "It's a boy!" written in blue. After dinner, she'd tell him that she had a special dessert and place the cupcakes in front of Tom.

Setting the table with special care, she found two votive candles and set them artfully in the center, then left to pick up Tom. She fishtailed twice on black ice on the way to Kinsey, which frightened her and reminded her to ask him if they could please get some new snow tires this weekend.

She pulled into the Kinsey faculty parking lot, looking at the double doors every two minutes until she saw Tom's blond head exit the building. Her heart leaped with a mixture of excitement and anticipation, and she said a quick prayer that she'd be able to get through dinner without spilling the beans. He deserved to find out about his child in a special and memorable way, not sitting in a parking lot. Taking a deep breath, she smiled as he opened his door and sat down beside her.

Immediately, she could tell something was wrong.

He didn't reach for her over the bolster and pull her as close as possible, kissing her breath away. Placing his briefcase on the floor, he buckled his seat belt before looking at her and offering a bland "hello."

"What's wrong?"

"Huh? Oh. Nothing, really. Just a lot on my mind."

"Tom, I can tell that—"

"Let's head home, okay?"

Forcing herself not to press him for answers was difficult, but she put the car in reverse and backed out of the parking space. They fishtailed immediately, and she whimpered as the car swerved close to another car.

"We need snow tires," she said. "How about this weekend?"

"Let's try to make do," he said. "It'd be over a hundred dollars for four."

"But the car keeps—"

"We don't have the money, Eleanora," he barked at her. "Just . . . just drive slower."

She hunched down in her seat, unaccustomed to him yelling at her.

"Sorry," he said as she pulled onto Main Street, headed toward home.

"I wish you'd tell me what's bothering you, Tom. A problem shared is a problem halved."

"My bank account's dwindling," he blurted out. "And my salary isn't enough to support us."

She felt an unaccountable sense of relief at his words. This was about money? Well, she'd never had much money anyway. She knew how to live frugally. "We'll just have to be more careful."

"Yeah, right," he said. "What if you get another sinus infection, or you crash the car into a phone pole, or . . ."

. . . find out you're pregnant.

The words felt thick and uncomfortable in her head as she turned to look at him while stopped at a stoplight.

". . . or anything," he continued. "We have no savings. I have a few hundred dollars in my account, Eleanora. We're barely scraping by, and it, well, it makes me nervous."

"I'll pick up more hours," she said. "I'm sure Mr. Jenk—"

He huffed loudly, interrupting her. "Can you please not do that? It makes me feel like total shit."

"What? Why?"

"Because I'm old-fashioned, and I want to support you."

"Well, you can't," she said baldly, starting to feel annoyed with him. It was one thing for him to be concerned about money. It was another for him to sideline her from helping.

"Great. Thanks for that."

"You're a brand-new teacher, Tom. You're still getting used to—"

"I don't need my wife supporting me!" he yelled, his eyes angry and narrowed.

Eleanora stepped on the gas, seething as she turned down their road and parked the car in their driveway. As soon as she cut the engine, she turned to him.

"You're being a jerk."

"And you're emasculating me."

"I'm your wife, not some princess on a throne. I don't need to be catered to. Can you see that I'd feel better if you'd let me help?"

He turned to her, his face hard. But underneath the rigidity, she saw frustration and worry. "Neville offered me some extra hours."

"Well, hey, that's good, right?"

"Is it?" he asked, rubbing his chin. When his eyes met hers, the hardness was gone, and misery had taken its place. "The hours would be from six at night until eight in the morning, six nights a week."

"What do you . . . ?"

It took a moment for his words to register, but when they did, they sucked the breath from her lungs. He was talking about working the night shift at the dorms. He was talking about being away from her for twenty-two of the twenty-four hours in a day, and it made her heart clutch. Suddenly, she understood his bad mood. He wasn't angry at her—he was angry at the situation. He was upset about the prospect of being away from her.

Eleanora placed her hand on his arm. "Tom."

He took a deep breath and sighed, his eyes sad. "It kills me to think of being away from you every night. But sunshine," he said, reaching up to palm her cheek, "we need the money."

"I think we could get by on what we make," she said softly, hating the idea of him spending almost every night away from her, money or not.

"I don't," he answered, dropping his hand. He gave her a sad smile before opening the car door and trudging up the walkway to the front door.

She watched him go, fear making her chillier than the storm clouds that had rolled in a couple of hours ago. In many of the love stories she'd read, writers had mentioned a honeymoon period, during which newly married couples were madly in love, making love every night and reaching for each other every moment. And after the honeymoon, they settled into real life and all its hardships. Is that where she and Tom were? Had their honeymoon ended?

And left without the exhilaration of belonging to each other, would their marriage survive?

She thought about the tiny baby growing inside her and squared her jaw. Yes, they would survive. Hell, yes. They just had to figure out how.

Tom shucked off his boots and hung up his cashmere coat in the front closet, peeking out the door to see her still sitting in the car, a thoughtful expression tightening her pretty face, and he hated himself for making her worry.

But Neville's offer wasn't one that Tom felt he could refuse. They needed the extra money desperately. He needed to feel like he could take care of her should some unexpected expenses crop up, and how could he do that on one thousand dollars a month?

His coat slipped from the hanger, and he picked it up, hanging it again, and again it slipped to the floor. Growling with anger, he threw the coat on the floor and yelled "Fuck!" just as his wife walked into the house.

"Tom," she said, her eyes darting to the hanger in his hand. "I'll hang it up. Why don't you . . ." She reached for the hanger, then bent down to retrieve his coat, and something about her gentleness, her patience, her faith in him, made hot tears sting his eyes.

"I'm sorry," he said, his voice thick with emotion as he stared down at the floor. "You married me for a million dollars, and I can't even buy you snow tires."

"Stop."

He shook his head, looking up at her, stunned—as he always was—by her beauty. "You could have had anyone."

"I wanted you," she said, blinking her eyes and sniffling softly.

Unable to bear the thought of making her cry, he pulled her into his arms, burying his nose in her hair and inhaling the sweet smell of his wife. "I feel like I'd die without you."

"Don't talk like that."

"I've never known . . . I mean, I'm a thirty-two-year-old man, and I've never known what it was like to struggle to make ends meet."

"It sucks, doesn't it?" she asked, flattening her palms against his chest as she relaxed against him.

"The worst." He kissed her head. "I love you so much, baby. I just want to take care of you. You gave up so much for me, and—"

She gasped. "I gave up so much *for you*?"

He nodded, leaning back to look down at her. "You left your home and your job. Meeting me and moving away meant losing your cousin. Yeah. You gave up your whole life for me."

"Tom," she said, tears spilling over the wells of her eyes. "You gave up *millions* for me. Your job. Your family. Your home. Your connections. Everything. I gave up a crappy life that I didn't even like that much. *You* gave up . . . everything."

"I'd do it all again," he said, knowing it was true. Knowing it was true even though they were down to a few hundred dollars and he was faced with the prospect of an awful second job to help make ends meet. "Every time, I'd choose you."

"I have to tell you something," she whispered.

He pulled her closer, resting his cheek against her hair, feeling some measure of peace despite the financial problems that hounded him. She was his and he was hers, and they'd figure it out. As long as they had each other, they'd find a way to make ends meet. He was sure of it.

"Go ahead."

He felt her gulp against his shoulder.

"Sunshine?" he asked.

She raised her head, her blue eyes twinkling with tears as she looked up at him. Her lips twitched like they wanted to smile but she wasn't sure she should.

"Eleanora, what is it?"

Her tongue slipped out to wet her lips, and she searched his eyes. "I . . . I'm . . ."

"You're what?"

"Tom, I'm pregnant."

He stared at her face—at her wet lips and glassy eyes, full of apprehension—trying to process those three, simple, life-changing words. Later, it would occur to him that you aren't in control of your eyes or your facial expression or, for God's sake, your words in a moment like that, which was why Tom would be eternally grateful to God in heaven and every star in the sky that when he was finally able to draw breath, he started . . . laughing. Laughing and holding her tight and swinging her around in a circle of unadulterated happiness while looking down at her relieved face.

"How do you know?" he finally asked, feeling breathless and electric as he reached to cup her face.

Beaming back at him, she answered, "Haven't you noticed, I've never . . ." Her cheeks colored. "I've never had a period since we've been married."

No, it hadn't actually occurred to him. He'd just lived in the bliss of having her whenever he wanted her and hadn't questioned his good fortune. He counted back quickly in his head, raising his eyes to hers.

"Seven weeks?"

She nodded. "About that."

"Christmas Eve," he said softly.

She shrugged. "I don't know for sure, but the test only works after six weeks, so . . ."

"The test?" He hated the way his anxiety about money rose up again. "You've seen a doctor?"

"No, not yet. I took at test at work today."

"But you need to see a doctor. You're going to need . . ." He blinked his eyes against the burn of happy tears. ". . . vitamins or diapers or, God, sunshine, I don't know. Stuff. Babies need lots of stuff, don't they?"

She giggled. "Doctor? Soon. Diapers? Not until September."

"Hey! I'll have health insurance by then."

She placed her palms on her tummy, smiling down at them. "Good timing, little one."

And suddenly it struck him again: there was a baby inside her. A tiny person whom he and Eleanora had made together. "Can I . . . ?"

"Tom," she whispered. "Of course you can."

But instead of covering her hands with his, he dropped to his knees before her and leaned forward, pushing up her turtleneck and pressing his lips to the warm skin of her stomach. He closed his eyes, breathing in the clean scent of his wife, knowing a gratitude he'd never felt before—not ever in his entire life.

Her hands landed gently in his hair. "You're happy about it, Tom?"

He nodded, kissing her soft skin again, whispering in a hushed, almost reverent tone, "I'm happy."

After they celebrated with their fancy dinner and festive cupcakes, they went to bed, lying side by side, staring at each other in the darkness. Eleanora reminded him of what he'd told her in Las Vegas—that he was a little jealous of the Swiss Family Robinson, with all those brothers, and how he'd said that he wanted a "gaggle of kids" of his own someday.

"The gaggle has officially started," she said, covering his hands, which were resting against the bare skin of her belly.

"I was on the fence before," he said, his voice determined, "but I'm not anymore. We need the money, baby. I have to take the job."

"I know," she said sadly. "But I'll miss you."

"I'll be home for dinner every evening before I go back for the night." He sighed, kissing her neck. "Aw, I hate it, too. But you've got to see a doctor, and I don't want you working anymore."

"Tom—"

"I mean it. What if you slipped on the ice and fell? No, Eleanora. I mean it."

"I'm not a china doll."

"You're mine, and I need to keep you safe."

"I'll stop working when a doctor tells me to stop," she said firmly but gently. "I promise."

He huffed softly, then touched his forehead to hers. "It feels like a miracle."

"Or a dream?" she asked.

"If it's a dream, I never want to wake up," said Tom, kissing her nose.

"My life began the day my cousin followed me to the kitchen and asked for the name of my favorite poet." She nestled closer to him. "If it's a girl, I want to name her Elizabeth, and if it's a boy, I want to name him Barrett."

"Beth or Barrett? Are those the names you've chosen, sunshine?"

"Uh-huh," she said. "As long as their daddy agrees."

Daddy.

He gasped softly, letting the newness of the word settle around him. He was going to be a father, someone's *daddy.* And suddenly, it was the most beautiful word he'd ever heard in his entire life. He'd had a very formal grandfather and an unhappy, distant father, never a *daddy*—never the playful, familiar nickname for someone who was supposed to love you from the very day he found out you were coming.

His voice was gravelly and thick in his ears when he answered, "He agrees."

Then he pulled his wife into his arms and buried his face in her hair, letting the deep well of emotions inside his heart have their way with him.

They fell asleep like that, tangled together, a mix of hopes and dreams, miracles and worries, gratitude and wonder, and love.

Eleanora woke up early, and, careful not to wake up Tom, she shrugged into her bathrobe and slippers and tiptoed from their room, heading downstairs to make coffee. But downstairs, she realized as she turned on the coffeemaker, was freezing, and she turned up the thermostat before taking Tom's cashmere coat from the front closet and putting it on over her bathrobe. It smelled like him, like warm man and spicy aftershave, and she closed her eyes for a moment, memorizing the smell as one of the best in the world.

Somehow they'd survived last night—their first minifight in the car and her earth-shattering news—and instead of pulling them apart, it had knitted them back together.

Slipping her hands into the pockets of his coat, she found a folded letter, which she withdrew as she walked back into the kitchen to wait for the coffee. She unfolded it, smoothing it on the kitchen table. It was addressed to Tom, and the return address was Haverford Park, Haverford, PA.

A letter from Tom's grandfather.

She sucked in a breath and turned it over. The seal hadn't been broken.

The coffeemaker hissed, and she jumped up, leaving the letter on the table and pouring herself a cup of hot coffee, then leaning back against the counter. She eyed the letter as if it were a snake and took a scalding-hot sip of coffee.

Why was Tom carrying around an unopened letter from his grandfather?

And why did Eleanora have the most overwhelming desire to open it up and read it?

And if she opened and read it, would she somehow be violating Tom's trust?

Chewing her lip, she sat back down at the table, placing her palm over the letter and sliding it closer. She turned it over, looking at the strong, bold cursive that addressed it.

Picking it up, she rapped it against the tabletop for a second, then put it back down.

It was none of her business. Whatever the letter said, Tom had decided not to open it, and she needed to respect that.

Except, she thought, flicking a quick glance down at her stomach, hidden under her nightgown and bathrobe, the baby she carried was an English. A very, very tiny English, of course, but an English nonetheless.

Eleanora had bid farewell to her family the day she left Romero. She hadn't heard from them since, and they hadn't heard from her, and though she hoped that they'd have fruitful and happy lives, she wouldn't be reaching out to them anytime soon. Evie had been her only family, and Evie was gone, far away in Hong Kong, where she was building her own life.

On the other hand, Tom's family—a controlling, crotchety grandfather, a weak-willed father, and a half brother

Tom barely knew—such as they were, were in Philadelphia. Not so far away. Close enough to be, well, *family* . . . if they could all learn to get along.

And didn't she owe it to her baby to try to get along, to try to make peace with her husband's family?

She sighed as the thought—*Your husband's family is very rich*—fluttered through her head, and she checked her motives. *You're not doing this for money, are you?*

Biting the inside of her cheek before taking another sip of coffee, she swiftly came to the conclusion that no, she wasn't. Unlike Tom, who'd grown up in luxury, Eleanora had grown up with nothing. She'd started working at fourteen years old. She'd eaten SpaghettiOs for Christmas dinner. She'd made do with hand-me-downs until they were threadbare. Eleanora wasn't frightened of poverty, and she certainly didn't know what she was missing by not having Tom's inheritance.

Tom, on the other hand, was suffering. Yes, he was doing his best, and yes, she knew that he would do anything in order to keep her and Beth or Barrett safe and happy. But if they could make amends with the Englishes, not only would their child know his or her family as a by-product of reconciliation, but Tom could stop worrying so desperately about making ends meet. He wouldn't have to take the second job at Kinsey. He wouldn't snap at her when she picked him up, with the stress of money weighing him down. He wouldn't doubt himself and beat himself up when he couldn't afford snow tires. He could resume the life he was meant to live before he'd married her.

Sighing deeply, her lips twitched as she slipped her fingernail into the seam of the envelope and ripped it open.

February 1, 1982
Haverford Park

Dear Tom,

There is no easy way to begin a letter like this, especially when writing to one's grandson from whom one is estranged. Best cut to the chase. My health is in decline. I was diagnosed with cancer just after Christmas. I've been advised that I don't have more than six months to live.

It's cold reality that we all must step up to the life eternal at some point, and my time comes quickly now, Tom. I know you see me as a flinty old bastard, but I'm also a man who needs to make amends before his time is up.

When you introduced me to your wife in December, I was hard on you, and on her. I was certain that you'd married her solely to secure your inheritance, and that once in hand, you'd divorce. I thought I smelled trickery when she walked into my office, so much younger and less sophisticated than the other women you'd dated. I expected that when I cut you off, you'd get rid of her quickly and take me up on my offer for more time. I never thought you'd choose her over family. I never thought you'd choose her over money.

You're not a bad man, Tom, but life has been handed to you on a silver platter in many ways. Your expenses have always been paid, your schooling and college a gift from me. It's not that you squandered your gifts, but you never seemed to take yourself very seriously, glad-handing instead of working, skiing the slopes instead of hunkering down at your desk. I worried I'd created a playboy. I hoped that the love of a good, stable woman could turn you around.

Turns out, I was right. It was this girl from Colorado whom you barely knew, who I assumed was a ringer, who somehow made you grow up. You turned your back on the easy life: on Haverford Park, on your father, on me, and, most remarkably, on your trust, in order to keep her in your life. I know that you are teaching at dear old Kinsey to support her, and for the first time in my tired old life, I know a feeling of true pride when I think of my oldest grandson.

You will recall that all I ever wanted was for you to find a good woman who'd make you honest, make you hardworking, and make you true. Turns out, this little waitress from Vail was the ticket. Old fool that I am, I just didn't see it.

When you're ready to return to Haverford Park with your bride, I will be ready to welcome her into our family. I will only be sorry I don't have more time to get to know her and to see your marriage to her deepen and flourish.

Please come soon, Tom.

Your,
Grandfather

By the time Eleanora finished reading, the letter was dotted with teardrops and her coffee had grown cold. Glancing up at the kitchen clock, she saw that it was not even six yet, which meant that Tom would be asleep for another hour, at least.

Wiping her nose with the corner of her bathrobe, she stood up from her seat and found pen and paper in a kitchen drawer. Then she sat back down at the table and started a letter of her own.

Chapter 17

Two weeks into his stint as resident adviser for the sophomores at Cambridge Hall, Tom wouldn't exactly say that he enjoyed his second job—and being away from Eleanora almost every night was sheer hell—but he felt satisfaction in knowing that he was providing for her and Beth or Barrett.

She'd been to see an excellent obstetrician in Litchfield this week, who estimated her pregnancy at eight weeks and gave her a due date of September twenty-first. Tom was relieved by this news, because if he *was* rehired for the next school year, he'd have health insurance by August and enough of a raise for their bills to be slightly less worrisome.

Things weren't perfect, but they were looking up, and Tom felt proud of taking responsibility for his life: for his wife, his marriage, his job, and his child. It wasn't a flashy life, but it was his—totally self-made, with the help of his beloved—and that made him feel good about it.

Which is why Dean Gordon's news on Sunday morning was so unwelcome.

"Tom!" shouted Neville from across the quad.

Tom was hurrying to his car. It was 8:01, and he was headed home to Eleanora. He'd wake her up by making love to her, and then they'd have all day, and, more importantly, all night, together.

"Hello, Neville!" he called, opening his car door and shoving his duffel bag of dirty laundry in the passenger seat.

"Glad I caught you before you headed home. Good news! We hired a new man for phys ed, and he'll be moving into Cambridge on Monday!"

Tom felt his face fall. No, he didn't love sleeping across town from his wife, but working two jobs was padding his bank account. He *needed* this job.

"Oh no," said Neville, reading Tom's expression. "I thought you only wanted it to be temporary."

"I did. I . . ." He paused, looking down at the ground before flicking his gaze back up to Neville's sorry eyes. "Eleanora's pregnant. The money was, well, I was glad to have it."

"Tom! Well, that's smashing news!"

"Thank you, sir," said Tom, unable to keep a smile from breaking out across his face.

Dean Gordon winced. "But I've made a terrible mistake. I'll, uh, I'll tell Mr. Gibbons that we don't need—"

"But we *do* need a phys ed teacher," said Tom. "And room and board at Cambridge are part of the job."

"Maybe we could find him off-campus housing, or . . ."

Tom reached out and put his hand on Neville's shoulder. "No, sir. It's all right. Perhaps I can find something else."

"If it's any consolation, I will be recommending to the board that you are hired as our full-time English teacher this fall, Tom. You've been just terrific with the boys."

Tom brightened a bit. It wouldn't help them now, but it would be a relief to have health insurance when the baby came. "Thank you, sir. That's great news."

"Is it?" Neville smiled at Tom amicably, but his expression was thoughtful. "Do you like teaching, Tom? Is this where you belong? At Kinsey? I know that we were a bit of a haven for you in December, when you first arrived. But taking on this lifestyle is a choice, and I hope you'll do some thinking before June, when you're offered the position. It's not for everyone, and I'd hate to see you land here by default when your destiny lies somewhere else."

"Where else, sir?"

"You were in finance, weren't you? Working with your father and grandfather?"

"Yes, I was."

"Don't you miss it?"

Tom shrugged. It felt like another lifetime, so very far away from where he was now, working in Cornwall, Connecticut, living in Weston, with his wife and a baby on the way. But, to be fair, parts of him *did* miss it. He missed the income and security, certainly, but he also missed the deals and the travel, the opportunity to effect major change, to buy and sell companies, the thrill of the deal. Yes, he missed it, he admitted to himself. But it wasn't an option for him. So he'd better make his peace with teaching.

"My life is here now," said Tom.

"Well, we're happy to have you, Tom. Oh, say, did I tell you that Charity and Geoffrey patched things up?"

Poor Geoff.

"Yes, indeed. Wedding's back on for May."

"Congratulations, Neville. That's fine news."

Neville nodded happily as he turned to walk away. "Say hello to Eleanora for me, will you? And best wishes to both of you."

"Will do. And thank you, sir."

So he'd lost his second job, but he'd be hired on full-time. He thanked God that he wouldn't have to sleep apart from his wife anymore and just hoped they could make ends meet until August. They could. They would. He would do whatever he needed to do to make it happen.

As Tom drove home, his mind wandered back to Neville's words: *I'd hate to see you land here by default when your destiny lies somewhere else.*

Tom English's destiny, of course, had always been at Haverford Park, working for English & Son. But he'd rather taken it for granted, hadn't he? He hadn't poured his all into English & Son the way he'd given his all to Kinsey. What if he had? What if he had knuckled down and worked hard? What if he'd had Eleanora by his side to cheer him on and keep him focused?

His face hardened. There's where the fantasy ended. Eleanora wasn't welcome in his old life, which meant his only option for the future was this life, here at Kinsey, where they were both welcome and respected. So be it.

Turning into his driveway, Tom was shocked to find a limousine parked out in front of his house, and even more shocked when he saw the driver, Smith, behind the wheel. Young Smith was his grandfather's newly hired driver, which meant that . . .

No. No! Why would his grandfather be here? Alone with Eleanora? Good God, what the hell was he saying to her?!

God only knew what venom would be spewing out of his grandfather's mouth. Tom's heart clutched as his car skidded to a halt, and he raced into the house.

"Eleanora?"

"In here, Tom!"

He strode to the kitchen and came to a bewildered stop in the doorway to find his grandfather and his wife sitting together at the kitchen table across from each other, drinking coffee like long-lost best friends.

His eyes darted to Eleanora, who rose from her seat, holding out her arms to him. She looked happy and serene, he was relieved to discover, but as Tom crossed to her, he kept his eyes on his grandfather's bowed head. Pulling Eleanora into his arms, he kissed her cheek distractedly.

"What's going on here?"

"Your grandfather's come to visit."

"I see that," he said. "Why?"

She leaned up on her tiptoes, brushing her lips with his, and Tom focused on her, finding her eyes both pleading and tender. "Listen to what he has to say?"

"Why should I?"

"Because I'm asking you to," she said gently.

Stepping out of his arms, she took his hand. She sat back down in her chair and tugged on Tom's hand, urging him to join them. Because he could refuse her nothing, he complied, sitting stiffly across from his grandfather, who finally lifted his sky-blue eyes to his grandson.

"Morning, Tom."

Tom nodded curtly. "Sir."

"I think your wife is . . ."

Tom braced himself, squeezing her hand, sitting up straighter and ready to throw this old man out of his house if he dared to insult Eleanora again.

". . . plucky as all hell."

"What?"

His grandfather grinned a short-lived grin. He took a deep breath, regarding Tom seriously. "I'm sorry I didn't give her a chance."

"You are?"

The older man nodded, then coughed—a dry, hacking cough that rattled his old bones. He put a snow-white handkerchief to his lips, and Tom noticed a smear of red when his grandfather pulled it away.

"I jumped to conclusions that, in fairness, were partially true. You married her for the money."

"Now wait a second," said Tom, but a squeeze of Eleanora's hand silenced him.

"It's the truth, Tom," she said. "We *did* marry for your inheritance."

"Originally. But . . ." started Tom.

"Love came quickly," said Eleanora, smiling tenderly at Tom, almost as though they were the only two people in the world. "*So* quickly."

"You married her to get the money, but you ended up falling in love with her," said his grandfather evenly. "I can see that now." He cleared his throat. "You'll forgive me, I hope, for wanting to test this whirlwind marriage. Mind you, I don't approve of such impulsive acts, but from what I can piece together, you're working hard here. Good, honest, true work. And that makes Eleanora English a good woman, Tom. A good woman for you."

"Yes, sir," he said, stunned by his grandfather's change in attitude.

"Plus, she's carrying the next English, isn't she?"

Tom's eyes darted to Eleanora's. "You told him?"

"Of course," she said. "He's family."

"Some family," said Tom, his anger rising. "You kicked me out of Haverford Park. You insulted my wife. You cut me off. You blackballed me. You—"

"I'm dying, Tom."

The slice of a blade.

The sharp, empty thwack of the guillotine.

The echo of a gunshot.

His grandfather's words landed in that company.

The air was sucked from Tom's lungs until they burned with emptiness, and he blinked his eyes several times in shock. "What? What are you talking about? You're as healthy as a horse."

"I'm dying, son. Cancer. I don't have much time left."

Tom inhaled deeply through his nose, wincing as he processed these words. His grandfather had never been a warm and fuzzy granddaddy figure in Tom's life, but he had been a stable, grounding force—a constant—and, in his own way, he had loved Tom.

"It's my lungs. Damned pipe smoking."

"Sir, I'm . . . I'm so . . ."

"Yes, yes. None of that, now." His grandfather cleared his throat, which brought on another coughing fit, and this time, the handkerchief was much redder when he pulled it away. "Ahem."

Eleanora leaped up and poured Mr. English a glass of water, placing it before him.

"Thank you, my dear."

Tom took her hand and wove their fingers together as he realized she was crying. She squeezed his hand, her eyes encouraging Tom to make amends.

His grandfather took a sip of water before continuing.

"I've released your trust. The penthouse is yours. Your job at English & Son is waiting. And when you're ready, I'd like to welcome you," he shifted his eyes to Eleanora and gazed at her warmly, "and your bride . . . home."

Home to Haverford Park.

Until that moment, Tom hadn't realized quite how much he longed for his old life, but his heart burst with such palpable relief, he closed his eyes against the wellspring of emotion it elicited. It was like coming to the end of a long, arduous race. He could finally go home again.

But Neville Gordon's face flashed through Tom's mind, and he shook his head. "I can't leave Kinsey in the lurch, sir. I have a responsibility to finish out the school year."

Tom expected his grandfather to try to strong-arm him into coming home, but he didn't. His papery-thin lips tilted up in a small smile, and he nodded his head. "Yes, sir, you do. And as an English, I'd expect nothing less than for you to honor that commitment."

It was the first time his grandfather had ever addressed him as "sir," and Tom felt a deep sense of satisfaction in knowing that, sitting here in this little kitchen in the middle of nowhere, with a wife his grandfather had originally rejected, Tom had finally made the grade in his grandfather's eyes. He was finally living up to the English name in a way that made his grandfather see him as an equal, and it made Tom's chest swell with pride.

"We can come down on the weekends, sir."

"I'd like that, Tom."

"So would I," said Eleanora, sniffling softly.

The elder English placed his hands on the table to stand up, and Tom rushed around the table to help him, holding his arm as they made their way out to the car.

Smith hopped out of the front seat and circled the old Daimler, opening the back door for Mr. English and grinning at Tom.

"Long time no see, Mr. Tom."

Tom smiled back at the chauffeur. "What you see is what you get, Smith."

Smith's eyes twinkled as he volleyed back, "You ain't seen nothin' yet."

"Oh, will you two knock it off?" demanded Mr. English as Tom helped him into the back seat.

He squatted down beside his grandfather, reaching for his wrinkled hand and clasping it tightly. "You going to hang on until September, old man? I want you to meet your first great-grandchild."

"No promises, Tom," said his grandfather. "But I'll try."

Tom swallowed the lump in his throat and nodded. "Take care of yourself."

"As long as you take care of *her*," said his grandfather, gesturing with his chin to where Eleanora stood on the front stoop, her hand raised in farewell. "Start by getting her a proper coat, damn it."

"Yes, sir," said Tom, patting his grandfather's hand before shutting the door and stepping away from the car, back to Eleanora.

He put his arm around her, lifting his own hand in farewell as the black limo pulled out of their driveway and drove away.

"I feel like I should ask how this happened," he said, looking down at her face.

"How about just be glad it did?"

"You reached out to him?"

"In a manner of speaking," she said, winding her arms around his neck. "I missed you."

"You're changing the subject."

"I can think of so many nicer ones that need our attention."

She pressed her breasts against his chest, and his thoughts scattered. Leaning down, he dropped his lips to hers and kissed her, somehow maneuvering them back inside the house and kicking the door shut with his foot.

When she was limp and loose, he drew back from her.

"He told me to buy you a new coat."

"I'll take it," she said, pulling his head back down for another kiss. "Let's go to bed."

"What a good idea," he said, letting her lead him up the stairs. "But tell me something, sunshine. One thing, okay? I need to know."

She turned at the head of the stairs and looked down at him. "Anything."

"Was it for the money?"

"What do you mean?"

"The money. Did you reach out to him because you wanted the money?"

Her eyes softened as she shook her head. "No, love. It was for Beth or Barrett. And for you." She sighed, reaching out to tousle his hair. "All I had was Evie. She was it. But she's so happy in Hong Kong, I need to face the fact that she's making her own life there, which leaves me . . . alone. But Tom, you *have* family. You have a grandfather, a father, and a brother. They're yours. They belong to you. And I want Beth or Barrett to have family, to have a legacy, to belong, so . . ."

"So you mended fences for me."

She nodded. "Forgive me?"

"I adore you," he said softly, stepping to the landing so he could sweep her into his arms.

"Do you know what you are, Tom English?" she asked him as he set her carefully on their bed and climbed over her.

"A dream come true?" he asked her, dipping his head to brush featherlight kisses to her throat.

"Exactly."

"Then I guess," he said, leaning forward to claim her lips with his, "that makes you my miracle."

EPILOGUE

Haverford Park
Christmastime 2015

"His miracle," sighed Valeria, grinning up at Eleanora from where she still sat cross-legged on the floor.

"I loved it," sighed Emily. "I love that Barrett brought you back to the Englishes."

"Glad he wasn't a Beth, huh?" asked Daisy, nudging her cousin.

"Heck, yes."

Jessica English, whose head was resting on Kate English's shoulder, sighed. "Is that where you got Alex's name? From Charity Atwell's brother?"

Eleanora grinned. "Subconsciously, maybe. He *was* devilish . . . just like Alex."

"Whatever happened to Evie?" asked Molly, tucked into the corner of the sofa, beside her friend Daisy.

"We lost touch for a while," said Eleanora, sipping her now-cooled cocoa. "But then Facebook happened! And we found each other again."

"Is she still in Hong Kong?" asked Daisy.

Eleanora nodded. "For over thirty years now. She and Van were married in 1984, and though Tom and I were invited, we couldn't go." She smiled back at Daisy. "Fitz was on the way."

"And then Alex, and Stratton, and Wes," said Valeria. "You had your hands full. No wonder you lost touch."

"Did my," Kate cleared her throat, "great-grandfather ever get a chance to meet Barrett?"

Eleanora's eyes misted a little. "He did. He was so tough, girls. He held on until Barrett was born and passed away two weeks later. I'll find a picture for you, Emily."

"You liked him?" pressed Kate, her voice tentative, like the answer mattered.

"I did. In the end, I liked him very much," said Eleanora, smiling at her niece. "And *your* father became an important part of the boys' lives too, Kate. And of course, so did you."

"What was in the letter you wrote to Tom's grandfather?" asked Jessica, leaning forward on the love seat.

Eleanora took a deep breath, hearing whispers from the past in her head. "It carried my dreams for a family. My hope for a miracle."

"You won't tell us?" asked Valeria, ever the straight shooter.

Eleanora shook her head. "No, girls. That bit stays between me and old Mr. English, bless his heart."

"Did you ever tell Tom about the letter?" asked Emily.

"I did. Years later, when it didn't matter anymore."

Molly sighed wistfully. "Thanks for telling us. It's a lovely story."

All the girls chimed in with their agreement, and Daisy applauded softly, which turned into full-blown cheers as the other girls joined in. In fact, it almost drowned out the sound of the front door opening.

"Ladies? We're home!"

Eleanora beamed at the sound of her husband's voice coming into the front foyer of Haverford Park. "In here, Tom."

Tom peeked his red cheeks into the room, flanked by Alex and Fitz, who grinned at their wives.

"How was your game?" asked Eleanora, referring to their annual neighborhood game of platform tennis over at Westerly, the Winslows' next-door estate.

"The Winslows whooped our asses," said Barrett, joining his father and brothers. "J.C. and Étienne played with me and Fitz. Dad played with Alex, Strat, and Wes."

"Yes!" cried Jessica Winslow English, raising her fists in victory. Then, catching sight of her husband Alex's surprised expression, lowered them sheepishly and sprinted across the room to kiss him.

"So Ten lost, huh?" said Kate, standing up and stretching with a grimace. "I'm due for supper at Chateau Nouvelle. See you all later?"

Her friends and family kissed her good-bye, waving as she slipped out of the living room.

"Is anyone hungry?" asked Eleanora, smiling at her gaggle of sons. "Because I believe breakfast-for-dinner is ready."

Emily, Daisy, and Valeria stood up and grabbed their men en route to the dining room, led by Jessica and Alex. Molly lingered for just a moment, holding out her hands to Eleanora, then leaning forward to kiss her future mother-in-law's cheek.

"Thank you again for telling us," she said. "It was a wonderful story."

"You're welcome," said Eleanora, flicking her glance to the foyer entrance, where Tom and Weston looked on. "I think someone's waiting for you."

"And for you," said Molly, dropping Eleanora's hands and turning to her fiancé, Weston, who took her hand and led her toward the dining room.

Tom took off his caramel-colored cashmere coat, laying it over the back of the couch as he approached her, his hair more white than blond now, his face weathered, his smile just as handsome as it was on the day he asked her the name of her favorite poet in a Colorado diner. He held out his arms, and she slipped into them, as she always had, as she always would.

Taking a quick look, to be sure no English brothers lingered in the vestibule, he kissed their mother soundly, stealing her breath, as he had a million times before.

"Good evening, sunshine?" he asked, grinning down at her.

"The best," she answered. "They're wonderful girls."

"You raised wonderful boys," he said, kissing her again.

"I love you tons."

"I love you back."

She looked behind him at the decorated Christmas tree.

"It's our thirty-fifth," she said, smiling up at him.

"And every one better than the last."

She touched his cheek tenderly. "I saved the last one for you."

He grinned as he let her go, watching as she reached for one final ornament, waiting on the mantel, and handed it to him.

Tom looked down at the cut-glass ornament in his hands, reading the words Eleanora had had engraved on it for their second Christmas together, when Barrett was just three months old.

You and me ~ a dream and a miracle.

"We were," he said, gazing at her timeless loveliness before hanging the glass carefully on the highest branch.

"We *are*," she whispered, kissing him once more before taking his hand and following their gaggle of sons into dinner.

THE END

The World of Blueberry Lane continues with ...

THE WINSLOW BROTHERS

(Part II of the Blueberry Lane Series)

Bidding on Brooks
The Winslow Brothers, Book 1

Proposing to Preston
The Winslow Brothers, Book 2

Crazy about Cameron
The Winslow Brothers, Book 3

Campaigning for Christopher
The Winslow Brothers, Book 4

Turn the page to read a sneak peek of *Bidding on Brooks*!

Chapter 1

"Please, Skye. Just listen. You're the perfect person for this.
You've got to help me out."

Skye Sorenson rolled her eyes at Brooks Winslow, adjusting the brim of her baseball cap as she swept past him,
headed down the dock for her next job.

"I mean it, Skye. I'm up a tree . . . and we're friends. Can't
you give me a hand?"

Dreamy Delight needed a new float switch and bilge
pump, which would be difficult to manage with Brooks
Winslow standing on the dock, looking casually gorgeous
as he yammered at her about some charity event he wanted
her to attend.

Looking down at her hands, she noted they were still
covered with engine grease from the oil change she'd just
handled on the outboard motor of a J-24 sailboat. Not wanting to get black fingerprints on the white fiberglass of the
motorboat she was about to service, she took a bandana
out of the back pocket of her overalls, then turned to face
Brooks as she wiped her fingers.

"Are you going to follow me around all afternoon if I don't
listen?"

"Umm . . . pretty much."

She sighed with feigned annoyance. "Fine. You have my attention. Tell it to me again."

Brooks looked relieved and gave her a small grin that— *damn it*—made Skye's stomach flutter.

"Knew you wouldn't let me down."

"Haven't said yes to anything yet," she said, shoving the bandana back into her pocket and crossing her arms over her chest as she looked up at him.

"My sister, Jessica, is back in Philly this summer to get married, and to keep busy, she's organized some big benefit for the Institute of Contemporary Art. She and her girlfriends thought it would be fun to volunteer their single brothers to be auctioned off."

"Auctioned off?"

"Yeah . . . a bachelor auction."

"Some sister," said Skye, unable to keep the teasing from her voice.

"It's for charity," he said defensively, running a hand through his waves of jet-black hair.

"Okay. So you got roped into it." She thought back to an old movie she'd seen once where women were auctioned off as dates. At each of their feet had been a pretty lunch basket, and the man who was the highest bidder won a homemade lunch with the girl of his choice. "What do you have to do? Have lunch with someone?"

"Oh, no," he said with irritation, pursing his lips. "Nothing that painless. Jess wants to make money. *Big* money. She had to think bigger than lunch."

Skye stared up at him. "Dinner?"

"Nope."

"Two dinners?"

"Uh-uh."

She gestured to the sleek Sportscruiser moored at the end of the dock that she was supposed to be working on. "I'm out of guesses, Brooks . . . and that pump isn't going to fix itself, so—"

"A sail. She's auctioning off a sail. With me."

"Well, I don't know why you're complaining. You love sailing. You love women. What's the problem?"

Skye tilted her head to the side, looking at Brooks' way-too-handsome face with a cheeky grin.

Long ago, Skye had accepted the fact that Brooks would never see her as anything but a great mechanic, a proficient sailor, and a longtime friend. And she was—honestly and truly—satisfied with that status quo between them. He was rich and powerful—an ex-Olympian and world-renowned sailor from Philadelphia, while Skye lived a much quieter life, working as a "handyman" at her Dad's marina in Maryland. What they had in common was a deep love of boats, and that was just enough to keep their friendship intact.

The first time Skye had ever seen Brooks Winslow was the day he came down to her father's marina to claim the fifteen-foot Primrose wood-hulled sailboat gifted to him from his parents for his fifteenth birthday. He swaggered into Sorenson Marina, flashing his perfect smile at her, and her ten-year-old heart had grown wings as she'd discreetly followed him down the dock. She was instantly infatuated with Brooks, of course, but much more, Skye harbored a deep devotion to his Primrose, the most beautiful little double-ended Daycruiser she'd ever seen. Her stomach had been in knots as she walked behind him from a discreet distance, hopeful that he would handle the little sailboat with the grace and care she deserved. But Skye's worries turned out to be unfounded. He'd treated that pretty boat with respect and skill, and Skye had breathed deeply with relief, her eyes dewy with hero worship, as he sailed away.

Twenty years later, Skye knew for certain that Brooks was one of the most talented, natural, organic sailors she'd ever met in her life. Heck, he'd made it all the way to the Olympics and come home with a medal to prove what Skye had always known: any boat was safe in his hands, and she respected him more than most of the sailors she knew.

"Not a one-day sail," Brooks continued in a terse voice, jettisoning her memories as he prompted her back to their conversation. "Not even two. Jessica signed me up for a cruise. From Baltimore to Charleston."

Skye felt her eyes widen as she stared at him. "That's a week. Minimum."

"Yeah."

"Crew?"

Brooks grabbed the back of his neck with his hand, rubbing. "Nope. It's supposed to be . . . romantic."

A romantic cruise. For a week. Alone. With Brooks.

Lucky girl, she thought, ignoring the ridiculous spike of jealousy that jabbed a little at her heart and made her feel instantly guilty.

She couldn't help her attraction to him, of course, but the fact that it was totally unreturned made it manageable in a way that didn't hurt—and it wasn't like she had *feelings* for Brooks beyond friendship. She just liked looking at him. For Pete's sake, her eighty-year-old granny's heart would flutter at the sight of Brooks' thick, dark hair, flashing sea-green eyes, square jaw, muscular body and perennially tan hands that handled a boat with the same finesse that he probably handled his women. Noticing Brooks' good looks didn't make Skye unique or special, and it didn't mean she wanted more from him than friendship, either. It just made her human.

"Romantic," she murmured. Turning away, she looked out at the harbor where sailboats bobbed up and down in afternoon sun.

"Yeah."

"But you won't know who she is," said Skye, "until she wins you."

"Bingo," he said.

"And then you'll be trapped at sea."

"Precisely."

"She could be *anyone*."

"Yep."

"Does your sister really hate you?"

Brooks scoffed. "No. But she really loves modern art."

"Okay. Yeah. It's a pretty sucky situation. But how can I help?"

He grinned at her. "You can bid on me."

Look for *Bidding on Brooks* at your local bookstore or buy online!

Other Books by Katy Regnery

A MODERN FAIRYTALE
(Stand-alone, full-length, unconnected romances inspired by classic fairy tales.)

The Vixen and the Vet
(inspired by "Beauty and the Beast")
2014

Never Let You Go
(inspired by "Hansel and Gretel")
2015

Ginger's Heart
(inspired by "Little Red Riding Hood")
2016

Don't Speak
(inspired by "The Little Mermaid")
2017

Swan Song
(inspired by "The Ugly Duckling")
2018

ENCHANTED PLACES
(Stand-alone, full-length stories that are set in beautiful places.)

Playing for Love at Deep Haven
2015

Restoring Love at Bolton Castle
2016

Risking Love at Moonstone Manor
2017

A Season of Love at Summerhaven
2018

ABOUT THE AUTHOR

USA Today **bestselling author Katy Regnery** started her writing career by enrolling in a short story class in January 2012. One year later, she signed her first contract for a winter romance entitled *By Proxy*.

Katy claims authorship of the multi-titled Blueberry Lane Series which follows the English, Winslow, Rousseau, Story and Ambler families of Philadelphia, the five-book, best-selling A Modern Fairytale series, the Enchanted Places series, and a standalone novella, *Frosted*.

Katy's first Modern Fairytale romance, *The Vixen and the Vet,* was nominated for a RITA® in 2015 and

won the 2015 Kindle Book Award for romance. Four of her books: *The Vixen and the Vet* (A Modern Fairytale), *Never Let You Go* (A Modern Fairytale), *Falling for Fitz* (The English Brothers #2) and *By Proxy* (Heart of Montana #1) have been #1 genre bestsellers on Amazon. Katy's boxed set, The English Brothers Boxed Set, Books #1–4, hit the *USA Today* bestseller list in 2015 and her Christmas story, *Marrying Mr. English*, appeared on the same list a week later.

Katy lives in the relative wilds of northern Fairfield County, Connecticut, where her writing room looks out at the woods, and her husband, two young children, and two dogs create just enough cheerful chaos to remind her that the very best love stories begin at home.

Sign up for Katy's newsletter today: http://www.katyregnery.com!

Connect with Katy

Katy LOVES connecting with her readers and answers every e-mail, message, tweet, and post personally! Connect with Katy!

Katy's Website: http://katyregnery.com
Katy's E-mail: katy@katyregnery.com
Katy's Facebook Page: https://www.facebook.com/KatyRegnery
Katy's Pinterest Page: https://www.pinterest.com/
    katharineregner
Katy's Amazon Profile: http://www.amazon.com/
    Katy-Regnery/e/BooFDZKXYU
Katy's Goodreads Profile: https://www.goodreads.com/author/
    show/7211470.Katy_Regnery